D0628488

ASHES
TO DUST

WITHDRAWN FROM
ALBANY PUBLIC LIBRARY-MAIN
ALBANY, N.Y.

ASHES TO DUST

REX KUSLER

PUBLISHED BY

amazon encore

The characters and events portrayed in this book are fictitious. Any similarity to real persons, living or dead, is coincidental and not intended by the author.

Text copyright ©2010 Rex Kusler
All rights reserved
Printed in the United States of America

No part of this book may be reproduced, or stored in a retrieval system, or transmitted in any form or by any means, electronic, mechanical, photocopying, recording, or otherwise, without express written permission of the publisher.

Published by AmazonEncore
P.O. Box 400818
Las Vegas, NV 89140

ISBN-13: 9781935597599
ISBN-10: 1935597599

CHAPTER 1

"My daughter was murdered," he said. "Somebody bashed her head in with a baseball bat and burned her to a crisp out in the desert." He took in a breath, held it, and clenched his teeth, staring across the desk at Alice James. His eyes were red and swollen, his face bloated and pale. He was a big man, six-foot, barrel-chested, with wide shoulders. He appeared to be in his late forties. His hair was gray and cut short.

Sitting erect in her padded swivel chair, her fingers interlaced on the desk in front of her, Alice met his gaze. "I read about it in the paper, Mr. Roberts. I'm sorry. I can't imagine what you're going through."

Roberts nodded. "Well, shit happens. And then it happens again."

Alice offered a solemn nod, though she could only guess at his meaning. "And what is it we can do for you, Mr. Roberts?"

"Jack," he said. "That's what you can call me to start with. I don't like being formal."

"Alright, Jack." She waited.

Roberts swallowed and looked down at his hands where they lay resting in his lap. He blinked, fighting back tears. "It's been three days," he said. "The cops aren't doing anything. They're both a couple of morons—couldn't find their asses with both hands." He brought his eyes up and stared hard at Alice. "I want something done. I want that son of a bitch behind bars. I want to see some progress!"

"Three days isn't that long. A murder investigation can take months or even years—"

He nodded and then shook his head in disgust. "You too." He stood up. "I should have known as soon as I walked in here."

She looked up at him. "What is that supposed to mean, Jack?"

He put his hands on his hips. "That detective who gave me the name of your agency—James and James. I asked him if it was a father and son outfit or two brothers. He said no. Not even a brother and sister. He said, 'A white guy and a sister.' I thought he was joking, and when I walked in here a minute ago, I realized he was."

Alice's voice remained calm and even. "If you have a problem with the fact that I'm a black woman, I can easily step aside and let my partner handle the case. He has more experience than me as a former homicide detective—plus, like you say, he's a white guy."

Blowing out a breath, Roberts looked down at his cowboy boots. He shifted his gaze to the door, turned, and walked toward it. Placing his hand on the knob, he hesitated for a moment, then turned facing Alice. "Look. I'm sorry. I didn't mean what I said. I haven't been thinking straight since this happened. I haven't had a clear mind in twenty-six years. You want me to leave?"

Alice waved her hand toward the chair in front of her desk. "Have a seat, Jack," she said. "Let's talk."

Jim Snow lifted his beer mug from the soggy napkin that was stuck to the bar and took a drink. He swallowed, belched softly, and set the mug back down. He rested his elbows on the tarnished surface of the bar, his hands hanging limp in front of him, and studied the bartender where he stood in front of the sink washing glasses. He had a baby face, early twenties, short black hair, and a natural smile.

From where he sat at the corner of the bar, Snow had an unobstructed view of the entire area behind the bar, including the bartender's worn sneakers and the rubber mats covering the floor.

He glanced at his watch. Five ten p.m. He'd been sitting here for four hours. That was it—time to go. But what the hell, he thought. One more beer. He was contemplating the purchase of another pickled egg when his cell phone chirped. He stood up, dug it out of his front jeans pocket, flipped it open, and put it to his ear.

"Yeah, Alice. What's up?"

"Anything?"

"No." Snow shoved his barstool back, turned, and ambled unsteadily toward the men's room. "I haven't seen anything," he mumbled, keeping his voice low. "I never saw his hands go anywhere near his pockets, not even to get his comb out. All the money has gone into the cash register, his tips into the jar next to it."

"How much longer are you planning to stay?"

Snow pulled the door to the men's room open and stepped inside. It was small. The single stall, a sink, and two urinals were unoccupied.

He sighed. "Well, the client's paying for four hours. I was thinking of giving him an extra half hour as a bonus."

"Why?"

"The beer's going down good, and I'm going to have to take a cab anyway, so I figured one more can't hurt."

"How many have you had?" Alice asked.

"Six."

"Six beers in four hours?"

"What's wrong with that?"

"You're supposed to be working," Alice complained.

"I had to look normal. Blend in with the other customers. How often you see a guy walk into a bar and sit there nursing warm beer for four hours?" Snow turned his eyes to the urinal nearest the door, walked over to it, and unzipped his fly.

"You're in the men's room?" Alice said.

"Of course. You think it would be good to sit there in front of the bartender and discuss with you the surveillance I'm performing on him?"

"There's no one in the men's room with you is there?"

"I can't be sure. There may be someone in the stall, but if there is—he doesn't have any feet."

"Uh-huh."

"Alice, you seem to have lost your sense of humor. I think it's the stress of trying to make a go of this detective agency idea of yours."

"You thought it was a good idea when you agreed to join me."

"That was then. Now that we've been working at it for a while, it's starting to get old. I'm really sick of spying on people. I have to tell you, Alice, I've been thinking seriously about getting back into poker. I can feel my confidence returning."

"Really," Alice said. "When did that happen? After the third beer—or the fourth?"

"Now, see," Snow said, "this is another problem. You're starting to act like a wife. It's sort of like being stuck in a sexless marriage with—"

"Jim."

"What?"

"I'm not up to having this conversation at a time like this," Alice said.

"A time like what?"

"While you're half drunk, standing there dealing with nature's business."

"How do you know what I'm doing?" Snow said.

"I can tell by the tone of your voice."

"Oh." Snow chuckled. "Alice?"

"Yes?"

"I still love you. Will you come and pick me up?"

"I suppose I'll have to," she said. "I'll be there in twenty minutes. But don't drink any more beer. Have a cup of coffee and drink that until I get there."

"What difference does it make? We don't have anything else lined up. And you're just sitting there...unless..."

"Unless what?"

"You're feeling frisky?"

"Uh-huh. Like that's ever going to happen. The fact is we've got a big client. He just left."

"Is he over three hundred pounds?" Snow grinned.

"Get some coffee, Jim," Alice said. "I'll be there in twenty minutes."

CHAPTER 2

They drove in silence for the first couple of miles, Alice James at the wheel of her new Chevy Malibu. She wore a black business suit, matching the exterior color of her car. Her skirt had ridden up to mid-thigh, exposing a pair of long, shapely legs that highlighted her trim figure. At forty-one, she was still an attractive woman. Her straight black hair barely covered her ears, framing her unlined face. To Jim Snow she looked like a young supermodel.

Sitting in the passenger seat, breathing in the scent of fresh, new plastic, Snow could feel the fog lifting from his head. "I have to say, I do like your car. I've been thinking of trading in my Sonata and picking up one of these. A lighter color though. I don't think black is sensible for Las Vegas."

"It's my favorite color," Alice said. "It shows I mean business. Besides, these days cars come with air conditioners." She gave him a sidelong glance. "Would you like to stop by your house to change clothes?"

He turned his head to her. "You don't like what I'm wearing?"

"A T-shirt and blue jeans? Jim, you're forty-six."

Snow smoothed back his thinning hair. "Thanks for the reminder."

"I just think it would be better for business if we both dress professionally."

"We're private investigators," Snow said. "Not undertakers."

Alice shook her head and sighed. "Alright. Wear what you want. I'll try not to care."

Snow studied her face. Her eyes had narrowed; her jaw muscles were bunched in a knot. "I didn't know it mattered that much to you," he said. "Okay, we can stop by my place. I can iron a dress shirt and a pair of slacks."

"No, it's okay. Forget it."

Her right hand lay in her lap, her left on the wheel. Snow reached over and put his hand lightly onto hers. Her eyes widened, and her jaw muscles relaxed. "You know, Jim," she said, "sometimes you can be really sweet. Other times I feel like I could strangle you." She turned her face toward him and smiled. "You're a piece of work."

"I guess we should talk about that," Snow said.

"Your attitude?"

Snow shook his head. "No—work. What've we got?"

She braked for a light and said, "His name is Jack Roberts. He owns a convenience store in Barstow—"

"Barstow? I've never met anyone from there. Never thought of anyone actually living there. Every time I drive by that area, I get the feeling the whole town is vacant. Was he raised there? Or did he move there to start a business? Who would move to Barstow to open a convenience store?"

"I don't know, Jim," Alice said. "Those are questions I never thought to ask. His daughter's name was Laura. Her body was discovered burning in the desert near Stober Road off of Charleston, east of Red Rock Canyon. A motorist on an adjacent road saw the flames, called 911. By the time the fire truck got there, the body was smoldering and unrecognizable."

"Right," Snow said. "That was Tuesday night. If I remember correctly, from what I read in the paper, the victim's roommate came home from shopping, found the living room in disarray, and called the police."

"Yes," Alice said. "The body was so badly burned that the coroner had to ID the body from dental X-rays."

Snow turned his gaze to the front, watching the traffic pass in front of them through the intersection as he visualized a blackened corpse with a set of white teeth protruding from the shriveled skull. "So, how did this Jack Roberts from Barstow end up at our office door?"

"This is the part you may find hardest to believe," Alice said.

"What?"

"The lead detective gave him our names."

"Why?"

"Apparently, Mr. Roberts was dissatisfied with the progress the police were making. He threatened to complain to the section chief. The detective talked him out of that and told him that if he wanted to initiate his own investigation, he should hire someone. He recommended us."

"No kidding. Who's the detective?"

"You'll never guess," Alice said.

"Give me a hint," Snow said.

"Roberts called him a moron."

Snow chuckled. "Melvin Harris." He dug into his front jeans pocket and brought out his cell phone. He snapped it open and began to press the buttons. "I think we'd better meet him for coffee so we can thank him properly. What do you think?"

Alice smiled. "Yes. It'll be good to see Mel again—from the opposite side of the table."

Detective Mel Harris of Metro Homicide entered the coffee shop, grinning, his exaggerated swagger resembling a rooster on the prowl. Wearing a pin-striped dress shirt, open at the collar, and cotton slacks, his black hair was combed back and firmly cemented in place. Following closely behind, and ten years younger than Harris's forty-three, his junior partner wore a similar ensemble, along with a buzz cut. Their badges were clipped to the left side of their belts, their nine-millimeter handguns clipped to the right.

"If it isn't the odd couple," Harris said. "James and James." He approached the table Alice and Snow were seated at. As Snow stood up to shake his hand, he asked, "And which one are you?" He chuckled.

"Good one," Snow said. "Your wit seems to have sharpened since the last time I saw you."

Harris let go of Snow's hand and nodded, his grin spreading across his face. "Glad you noticed. I've been working on it." He put his hands on his hips. "I'm thinking about trying for a career move. Stand-up comedy."

"No kidding," Snow said. "What happened to the hamburger joint idea?"

"I like this one better. I've always had a knack for humor. Everybody always tells me that. Now all I need to do is expand on that—leave my mind open to funny stuff. When something hits me, I write it down. I'm still working on my first routine. Once I get it perfected, I'm planning to try it out on a live crowd. Test the waters." He turned his head to Alice, who was still seated at the table, her hand curled around her paper coffee cup.

Harris spread his arms. "No hug for your former partner?"

Alice offered a half smile and stood up, stepping around the table. Harris wrapped his arms around her, gave her torso a squeeze, and then turned to his partner, leaving one arm draped around her waist.

"She was the best partner I ever had," Harris declared. "We had our differences at times, but we worked together like a needle and thread."

Alice glanced at Snow and rolled her eyes. Shifting her eyes back to Harris, she said, "Yeah, it used to bother me at first— until I realized Mel needles everyone."

Harris's eyes popped wide. He pointed a finger at Alice and then reached into his front pants pocket and produced a small notepad and pen. He began to scribble. "I think I can use that," he said.

With paper and pen back in Harris's pocket, introductions were made to his junior partner. The two of them went to the counter and ordered, and then they returned to the table and sat down, each of them with a cup of foamy milk.

When they were seated, Snow reached across the table to Harris, offering a thin stack of folded twenties. "By the way," he said, "here's the two hundred I owe you."

Harris arched his eyebrows for a moment and then lowered them, smiling. "Oh yeah. Thanks." He took the bills and leaned back, shoving them into his pocket.

"That's the right amount, isn't it? Or was it more?"

Harris winked and offered a thumbs-up.

"I appreciate your referral," Alice chimed in. "I was a little surprised by it."

"No reason to be," Harris insisted. "You're both good detectives. We're all friends here. Besides, I was more than happy to get the guy off my back. He's a pain in the ass and a loose cannon primed to fire."

Snow frowned. "Why do you say that?"

"He's been on my butt twenty-four hours a day from the beginning of this investigation. Every two or three hours he calls me, wanting to know if we've arrested Miller yet. Threatening to go to the section chief and get me pulled off the case. Even alluded to the possibility of taking care of matters himself." Harris turned his head toward his partner for confirmation, who returned a solemn nod.

"Who is Miller?" Snow asked.

"Kevin Miller," Alice said. "He's the ex-boyfriend of the deceased. He was stalking Laura right up until the time of the murder."

Snow leaned forward, pulled his notepad out of his back pocket, and began to scribble.

Harris shot a look at Alice. "He wasn't stalking her," he snapped. "He was trying to win her back. No different than what he went through with her the other two times they broke up. They've always gotten back together; he had no reason to expect they wouldn't again. Everybody goes through that with women." He looked at Snow. "Right?"

Snow shrugged. "I don't know. I guess I'm different. I've never gotten back together with anyone I broke up with. There has to be a good reason for breaking it off in the first place, and nobody ever changes. They just act nice for a while, and then they get back to their usual self after they begin to feel comfortable."

Alice frowned and shook her head at Snow. "What was your good reason for breaking it off with me?"

Snow rolled his eyes. "We only had three dates, Alice. And I don't think this is an appropriate time or place to discuss our personal lives."

"Don't mind us," Harris interjected. "This is interesting. I'd like to hear the answer."

Snow met Alice's gaze. "It was just bad timing," he said, "plus, the fact that we have a great relationship. Why ruin it by getting involved with each other?" He turned his eyes toward Harris. "I look back over my life, and I realize the best relationships I've ever had were with the women I never dated."

Harris nodded and grinned. "You mean hookers?" He pulled his pad out and wrote it down, chuckling.

Alice took a sip of her coffee. "About Kevin Miller, Mel. So, you are investigating him. Right?"

Setting the pen down on his notepad, Harris looked up at her. "Of course. We questioned him, searched his house, and checked his truck for fibers, hair, and blood—with his permission. Found nothing. If you want my opinion—my gut feeling on this—I don't think Miller had anything to do with it."

"Who do you think did?" Alice asked.

"Off the record? I wouldn't toss out Laura's father as a possible."

"Why do you say that?" Snow asked.

"Just the way the guy is. The way he's been acting. He's almost in a panic to push us onto Miller. He's been acting kind of guilty."

"Do you have anything on him?" Alice asked. "Any motive?"

Harris shook his head. "It's still early. But if I were a betting man, I'd put my money on Jack Roberts. That's what my gut tells me."

"You have any leads yet?" Snow asked. "What about robbery?"

Harris looked at Snow. "Nothing was stolen. So it wasn't robbery, unless they changed their mind about taking anything after they clubbed her. Now, first off—you know I can't divulge anything that's confidential to the case."

"Is there anything confidential to the case?" Alice said.

"Nothing the lieutenant has told me to keep my mouth shut about. No. But you know I shouldn't even be sitting here discussing the case with you. I could get my ass in a sling for this. It was different with your brother-in-law's murder, Snow. He was your family. And we're family. We worked together. Am I right?"

"Of course," Snow agreed. "This isn't about the case. We're just friends having coffee together. Just shooting the bull."

Everyone nodded.

Snow leaned forward. "So what have you got?"

Harris took a sip of his latte and set it back on the table. He licked the foam from his upper lip and started in: "The neighbors didn't see or hear anything. The lab people checked the whole house and didn't find anything suspicious. No sign of forced entry, nothing out of place, except the end table and lamp that got knocked over when the victim fell. There didn't appear to be a struggle or any sign of sexual assault. The crime scene looked like the victim was caught by surprise. She might have put a hand up to try and block the blow, but the body was so badly burned that the coroner says there's no way to check for bruises or anything on the outside of the body. They did check for semen wherever they could internally and didn't find any. All he could tell me was there weren't any broken bones. Other than her skull.

"The lab people checked the victim's car pretty thoroughly—and the roommate's car. No signs of blood anywhere. No prints in the victim's car other than those of the victim and her roommate. That's to be expected; they were best friends and probably palled around together, shopping and stuff women do together." He took another sip of his latte and shrugged. "So we don't really have any hard evidence yet—except one thing."

"What's that?" Snow asked.

"Work boots," Harris said.

"Work boots? The actual boots?"

"No. Impressions. Size eleven and a half or twelve men's work boot prints in the dust leading from the side of the road to the body. The tread pattern was very clear—no attempt to try and cover them up. So my guess is the perp disposed of them after the murder."

Snow nodded and took a sip of coffee. "What was left of the body?"

"Like I said, not much, other than bones and teeth. And some partially broiled organs. It was burned beyond recognition. A motorist on another road nearby saw the fire from a distance. The body was engulfed in flames. It was about sixty feet from the side of the road. By the time the fire truck got there, it was almost out—and the baseball bat was nothing but a charred stump."

"The baseball bat?" Snow asked.

"The murder weapon," Alice said.

"Right," Harris continued. "It was on top of the body, along with the empty gas can sitting next to it on the ground. All of that was on fire."

Snow nodded. He looked at Alice. Their eyes met for an instant. Then they turned their attention back to Harris. "Anything else?" Snow asked.

Harris thought for a moment. "The boots," he said.

"What about the boots?" Alice asked.

"From the prints in the dirt, the crime scene analyst said it looked like they were fairly new."

CHAPTER 3

"Is it my imagination, or has Mel become less of an asshole?" Alice said.

They had left the coffee shop and were now driving eastbound along Charleston Boulevard in Alice's Chevy.

Snow stared at the passing buildings through the passenger window. "I've never thought of him in that regard. He's a little dense, but I've never had a problem with him."

"That's because you never had to work with him; you never had a chance to get to know him. And you're a man; he doesn't treat you the same way."

"Maybe." Snow turned his attention to her. "But it's also possible your perspective is colored...I mean biased."

Alice kept her eyes on the road ahead. "Sounded like a Freudian slip."

"It wasn't," Snow said. "But that's what I'm talking about. At times, you seem to have a chip on your shoulder, and I get the impression you may be looking for something that isn't always there. Not that I can blame you for that; I find myself doing the same thing when I'm with you."

"What do you mean?"

"I mean there are people who treat me differently because I'm with you. I don't notice it as much anymore, but I did in the beginning. Some of them glare at me, and others—women mostly—look at me with warm approval."

"Is that why you stopped dating me?"

Snow shook his head. "Of course not. I don't give a shit what other people think. I do what I want."

Alice smiled. "Then what was it?"

"How many times are you going to ask me that?"

"Until I get a valid answer."

Snow sighed. "Alright, let's just say I got a little scared."

"Because of me, or women in general?"

"Both. I've been through the ringer quite a few times—twice divorced. But it progressed to the third date. You invited me in. I thought, this is it—and to be honest, that old saying popped into my head."

"What old saying?" Alice said.

Snow grinned. "Once you go black, you never go back."

Alice nodded, smiling. "Well, that didn't hold true for my father."

Snow's grin faded. His eyes narrowed. "Your father was white?"

"That's what I'm told. I never met him; he left when I was six months old."

"Were he and your mother married?"

She emitted a short laugh. "You're kidding, right?"

"Your mother never got child support?"

"Oh sure. I will say that for the man. He does take responsibility for his actions. He sent money every month until my eighteenth birthday."

"Do you know where he's living?"

"Silicon Valley, California. He's the CEO of a high-tech company in Santa Clara. Deposition Technology, the second-largest semiconductor equipment manufacturer in the world. He's probably worth at least a few hundred million."

"You ever try to contact him?"

She threw Snow a scowl. "Hell no. I'm not going crawling to that sonofabitch. My number's listed. If he wants to reach out and touch my ass, he can call me. Besides, if I ever end up in the same room with him, I'm afraid I'd be tempted to knock his teeth down his throat. And that wouldn't be good for either of us."

Snow chuckled. "Hopefully you'll never get that mad at me."

Alice dabbed at the corner of her right eye with her thumb and then returned her hand to the steering wheel. "You'll never give me the chance."

Snow looked at his hands and said nothing.

"The thing is," Alice said, "neither of us is seeing anyone. I feel like it's kind of a waste if we don't spend some of our off hours together. Just as friends, maybe. Why be alone?"

Snow considered this for a moment. "I guess it couldn't hurt. If you don't mind being bored, you could come over once in a while. I like to enjoy my time off sitting in my underwear, drinking beer, watching baseball. How does that sound?"

"Tennis would be a nice alternative," Alice insisted. "And, I must say, I do have some attractive underwear." She smiled.

Snow chuckled. "Hmm, on second thought, I think we better institute a dress code. Or I may end up in California, sending child support payments to Vegas."

"You're not like that. You would never leave." Alice reached over and took his hand, interlacing her fingers between his. "I'm getting a little hungry. How about you?"

Snow nodded. "I've got a two-for-one coupon for the Boulder Nugget buffet. Shall we call it a date?"

Alice shook her head. "No," she said. "We're on the clock."

Snow was standing in front of the mashed potatoes when his cell phone chirped. He stepped back, pulled it out, and flipped it open. It was Jack Roberts.

"You having any luck?" Roberts asked.

"We're making progress," Snow replied.

"With Miller?"

Snow turned his head toward the carving station. The prime rib looked tender and moist, not much fat. He licked his lips. "We haven't talked to him yet."

"Why the hell not? He's the most likely suspect."

"That is true," Snow agreed. "But we find it more beneficial to our investigation if we gather the necessary information required prior to interviewing him. Otherwise, we won't know which questions to ask."

"Yeah, well, I guess that makes sense. When do you plan to interrogate him?"

"It probably won't be until tomorrow morning," Snow said.

"Shit," Roberts said.

"What's the problem, Jack?"

"That means I'll be up all night."

"Doing what?"

"Watching the bastard."

Snow sighed and looked down at his plate. His green bean casserole appeared to have lost its steam. "Where are you?" he said.

"I'm in my car, down the street from his house. I don't want him skipping town."

"If he were planning that, he'd have done it by now," Snow said.

"Maybe so, but I'm not taking any chances. If this was your daughter, what would you do?"

"I don't know," Snow said. "I've never had any kids. I'd like to think I would stay out of the way and let the professionals handle it. That's my recommendation to you."

"Then I guess you wouldn't understand," Roberts said. "She was all I had left, and now she's gone. I've got nothing left. All I can think about is setting this straight."

"Did you happen to bring a gun along with you from Barstow, Jack?"

There was no answer for a moment. Finally Roberts spoke. "I've got a handgun. It's in the trunk of my car, unloaded. It's registered and legal."

"That isn't reassuring to me," Snow said. "I hope you don't do anything stupid."

"Get the fucking guy behind bars, and you won't have to worry about it."

"Alright," Snow said. "We'll do our best."

"Good," Roberts said. "I'll be checking in."

Snow heard the connection clicking dead. He folded the phone shut and slipped it into his pocket.

Back at their table, he pulled his chair out, set his plate down, and seated himself across from Alice.

"You look troubled," she said.

"I am," Snow said. He sighed. "I just got off the phone with our client."

"And…?"

"I can understand why Harris shoved him off onto us. This guy's fuse is lit. I've got a feeling Kevin Miller will either end up in jail—or dead."

CHAPTER 4

At twenty-six, Crystal Olson was moderately cute. Her features weren't perfectly proportioned. Her nose was slightly oversized, her cheekbones lacked prominence, and her eyes were small. She had thin brown hair that fell to the middle of her back. Standing barely above five feet, her physique was that of a gymnast. Twenty years older, her hair cut to the middle of her ears, her mother, Kathy Olson, was an aging version of her daughter. She appeared to be in her late forties. Both women wore jeans and tennis shoes.

Alice James led them through the vacant reception area and down the short hallway to her office. Snow followed behind, rolling extra chairs down the hallway from his office, one stacked upside down on top of the other. Inside Alice's office he separated them and offered two of the four chairs in the room to the women.

He glanced around the room. "Anybody like anything to drink? We have coffee and water…?"

Crystal and her mother looked at each other solemnly, shook their heads without speaking, and sat down.

Snow cleared his throat, took out his notepad, and sat down next to Alice's desk. He looked over at her, then at Crystal. "So, you're staying at a motel for the time being. Is that right?"

Her hands folded together in her lap, leaning forward slightly, Crystal nodded. "They've sealed my home. We can't get in there without an escort while they're still investigating."

"Of course," Snow said. He turned his eyes to her mother. "Ms. Olson, are you from Las Vegas?"

She sat with her legs crossed, clutching her purse tightly in her lap with both hands as if it were a brick she was preparing to throw at him. "No," she said. "I'm from Omaha. I teach sixth grade there. Crystal called me after this happened, and I thought it best to fly down and offer my support and assistance." A hint of a cordial smile crossed her face.

"Did your husband make the trip?"

"I'm a widow," she said, and then she sighed heavily. "And that is one of the reasons I felt it necessary get down here as soon as possible—for Crystal—because this is the second time she has been forced to deal with this sort of tragedy."

"Oh," Snow said. "I'm sorry to hear that." He paused. "Your husband was in an accident of some sort?"

She sighed again. "No. In fact, he was murdered." She tilted her head back slightly as if to gain courage, and then she continued. "Crystal and I were in Grand Island, Nebraska, visiting my parents for the weekend. When we got back Sunday night, we found him. He had been lying in bed sleeping when it happened. The police said a steel pipe was used."

Snow's eyes narrowed. "That's terrible. Did the police find the person who did it?"

She shook her head and looked at her daughter, who was staring at the floor with damp eyes. "No. But they think it was probably someone he owed money to." She reached her hand up to her face and scratched her cheek with the edge of her thumbnail. Dropping her hand back into her lap, she turned her head to Alice. "You see, my husband was a drinker and a gambler. He had a terrible problem with it. I should have noticed the warning signs before we were married, but I was young and foolish, and I thought I could change him. And he got worse over the years. He only cared about himself and his own selfish, sick compulsions. Even the life insurance policy he had was pitiful—barely paid for the funeral. I had to borrow money from my parents for years after that because of our reduced income—and still, to this day, I haven't been able to pay them back. The entire ordeal was extremely depressing for both Crystal and myself." She turned her gaze back to Crystal. "Well, I shouldn't go on about that. It's in the past. Now we have this to deal with. I'm sorry for going on about it…"

"That's alright, Ms. Olson. I understand." Snow turned to Crystal. "So, Crystal, you moved here directly from Omaha?"

"Yes," she said. "I had been working as a cocktail waitress at a club in Omaha. The money from the tips was good, but I was getting bored with the Midwest and was curious about Las Vegas. I had heard you could make a lot of money as a cocktail waitress in the casinos. I wanted to experience the glitz and glamour of it. It sounded really exciting. So I moved here and found a job right away at Shillington's Casino. It's a few miles from the Strip, but they get a lot of the Southern California crowd and the locals from some of the better parts of town. You know, the Summerlin and Spring Valley areas. So the money has been good."

"How did you meet Laura Roberts?" Alice asked her.

"We had been working together at Shillington's Casino ever since day one when I got here four years ago. We became friends, and a year later I decided to buy a house in Summerlin. Laura owns an older home in North Las Vegas. She bought it before I met her. She was living there with her boyfriend. They broke up the first time about eight months ago, and he moved out. She didn't want to live alone, so she decided to rent it out and move in with me."

"Was that Kevin Miller she was living with?"

Crystal's eyes grew wide. "Yes, it was."

"As I understand it, they got back together afterwards?"

She nodded. "More than once. I mean, they were continually breaking up and getting back together. Though she never moved back in with him. She had been sharing my home since he moved out."

"When was their most recent breakup?" Snow asked.

Crystal looked up at the ceiling for a moment, then back at Snow. "I guess it was about three months ago. Around the middle of June."

"Is this the longest they've been apart?"

"Yes. In the past they always got back together within a couple of weeks. This time Laura was sure she wanted nothing more to do with him. But he wouldn't give up. He was constantly calling, leaving messages on our home phone, her cell phone. E-mailing her. Even stopping by unannounced wanting to talk to her, sometimes with a bouquet of roses. He was crazy about her. Obsessed."

"Did he have a key to your home?" Alice asked.

"I don't think so. I wouldn't have wanted Laura to give him one, but I have no way of knowing whether or not she gave him one—or if he had one made somehow." She shrugged.

"Do you think he might have killed Laura?" Snow blurted.

Mother and daughter exchanged wide-eyed looks. Crystal turned her head back facing Snow. "I guess it's possible."

"When was the last time he saw her?"

"I'm not sure. But the last time I saw him was Tuesday afternoon. He was coming up the walk toward the front door just as I was leaving home. It was a little after four."

Snow's eyes narrowed, and he adjusted his position in his chair, leaning forward and resting his forearms on his legs, his fingers interlaced. "Alright. Now, please go back to the beginning and tell us everything that happened that day."

"From the time I left work?"

Snow nodded. "Yes."

Crystal straightened in her chair, crossed her arms, and gazed at the floor. "I left the casino just before three p.m., an hour ahead of the shift change. I had a really bad headache, and the floor supervisor had shut down most of the table games in my section. So another waitress agreed to cover my area for the last hour of our shift.

"I got home around three twenty, and I found Laura in the living room watching television. We talked for a few minutes. Then I looked through my mail, changed clothes, and left the house to go shopping."

"The headache was better, I take it?" Alice asked.

Crystal brought her gaze up to Alice. "Just getting out of the casino helps most of the time. And getting out and doing something fun always helps me get rid of the tension."

Alice smiled and nodded.

Crystal returned a nervous smile and continued. "Anyway, as I was leaving home, I encountered Kevin Miller walking toward the front door from his truck, which was parked on the street in front of the house. Knowing that Laura wouldn't want to see him, I told Kevin that Laura wasn't home. I told him I didn't know where she was, and I didn't know what time she would be home.

"My car was parked in the driveway. I got in it and left, noticing as I drove away that Kevin Miller hadn't moved. He just stood near the front door, watching me leave."

"What time did you return from shopping?" Alice asked.

Crystal wet her lips and swallowed. She took in a shallow breath and continued. "It was around eight thirty. I parked in the driveway—"

"You always park in the driveway?" Snow asked.

"Yes," Crystal said. "There's a lot of stuff in the garage—only enough room for one car. Laura's car is fairly new, so I let her park in the garage. Plus she usually worked the swing shift; I work during the day. It's safer...for her." She looked down at the floor, pressing her lips together. Her mother reached over and put her hand on Crystal's arm.

"It's okay," Alice said. "Take your time. You can continue when you feel ready."

Crystal nodded, still staring at the floor. After a moment, her eyes wet, she looked up at Alice. "Alright. So I parked in the driveway. Came in through the front door. I walked into the living room, saw the lamp on the floor, the end table tipped over—right away I knew something was wrong.

"I ran upstairs and looked in Laura's room. I searched the entire house. I checked the garage and found her car parked there. Then I called the police."

Snow studied Crystal's face for a moment. "The police found the remnants of a baseball bat on top of the body. They believe it was the murder weapon."

Crystal nodded. "That's my bat. I play in a softball league. I always leave it next to the front door—for protection. You never know when you might need something like that."

CHAPTER 5

Kevin Miller was still up. They had called ahead of time to arrange an interview for the following morning. He would still be awake, he insisted, if they wanted to stop by anytime before midnight.

It was a few minutes after eleven p.m. when Alice and Snow arrived at his home in Henderson. As they pulled into Miller's driveway, their heads turned to the left, taking note of an older model Ford Thunderbird parked a half block away on the street. Framed in the glow through the rear window from the streetlight behind it, they could make out the silhouette of a man's head on the driver's side.

"Is that Roberts?" Snow asked.

"I never got a look at his car," Alice said, "but I would guess that's him."

Snow nodded. He cut the engine and set the brake. "I guess we should say hello."

They got out of the car and walked over to the Ford. The driver's side window was down. Roberts was sitting upright, his head leaning back against the headrest, his mouth agape. He was snoring softly.

"Mr. Roberts," Snow said as he approached the car.

Startled, Roberts jerked his head forward, then toward Snow. He closed his mouth and widened his eyes. His gaze shifted quickly from Snow to Alice and then back to Snow.

"Oh," he said. "It's about time."

Snow stuck his hand through the open window, shook Roberts's hand, and introduced himself.

"Now that we're here," Snow said, "why don't you get back to your motel and get some sleep?" Snow noted the bags under the man's eyes. "You look like you could use it," he said.

Roberts cleared his throat. "I was kind of hoping you'd let me tag along…you know…maybe I could be of some help to you."

"Sorry," Snow said, "we don't work that way."

"What if he decides to lie about something? I could point it out to you."

"There are a lot of reasons why it's a bad idea. I'm sure that if you think about it, you'll understand why it's best if you're not present while we're interviewing people."

Roberts clenched his teeth and shook his head emphatically. He pointed a finger at Snow. "Now look—I'm paying the two of you a hundred bucks an hour. That's a shitload of money. And this was my only daughter—dead." His lower lip quivered. He swallowed hard and blinked back the dampness filling his eyes.

Alice stepped forward and put her hand on the window frame of the car. Her voice soft and low, she said, "Jack, if you're not agreeable to our procedures, we'd be willing to step aside and let you find someone else to work for you."

Roberts nodded. "I hate to say it, but that's exactly what I'm thinking."

"Of course," Alice continued, "we would keep the retainer."

His eyebrows shot up. "Look, goddammit, I don't appreciate being threatened like that! Alright, I'm leaving. But I expect to see some progress." He reached up and turned the ignition key. The engine came to life. "And I want timely reports from you two—at least twice a day."

Alice smiled and removed her hand from the window frame. "Drive safely, Jack. We'll talk to you tomorrow."

"Yeah…fuck," Roberts muttered. Then he sped away from the curb.

Looking after the Ford, Snow said, "I have to admit, at times like this you are an asset to the partnership."

Alice looked at him. "You think so?"

"Yeah," he said. "If it were just me standing here dealing with that guy, I'm pretty sure I'd be minus a client right now."

"Is he still out there?" Those were the first words out of Kevin Miller's mouth as he opened his front door. Wearing baggy shorts and a T-shirt, he was six-foot, early thirties, with close-cropped black hair. His eyes were wide and bloodshot, his face pallid.

"You mean Jack Roberts?" Snow asked. "Yeah, he left. Don't worry about him."

"Don't worry about him? He's crazy—and I don't even have a gun."

"What's he done to make you say that?" Alice said.

"I could write a book, but I wouldn't know where to start."

"You mind if we come in?" Snow asked. He stood in the doorway with Alice behind him, peeking over his shoulder.

"Yeah, sure. Come on in. Sorry." He turned and crossed to the middle of the carpeted living room, then turned around. "Have a seat—wherever you like."

Alice and Snow chose the moss green sofa. Miller lowered himself unsteadily into the matching stuffed chair.

"How long have you known him?" Alice said.

Miller stretched his legs out in front of him and crossed his ankles. "Two years—as long as I've known Laura. Right from the start, she was dragging me over to Barstow with her to visit him. At least once a month. Every time we went there, it was like driving to hell."

"You mean because of the town itself?" Snow asked.

Miller shook his head. "No, it was the whole deal. This guy is like Satan, and he's living in hell. An hour after I met him, he pulls me aside and tells me I'm not good enough for his daughter and he wants me out of her life."

Alice leaned forward and interlaced her fingers in her lap. "What was the reason he gave?"

"He didn't like the way I look. I mean, that's exactly the way he put it. Then he told me he didn't like what I do for a living." He shrugged. "I'm a fireman. I thought these days every parent would like their daughter to marry a fireman. I mean, they can't all marry doctors."

"What does he have against firemen?" Snow said.

"He thinks all we do is sit around and eat—and sleep. Plus, he didn't like the fact that I'm at the station twenty-four hours straight. We work twenty-four on, forty-eight off; that's the way it is."

"So the situation never got better between the two of you?"

Miller shook his head. "Nah, it got worse. The guy hates me for some reason. He was always glaring at me, coming up with subtle insults, hitting me on the arm—hard. One time he wrapped his hand around my bicep and dug his nails into me. It even left a bruise. More than once I almost punched him, but I knew that's what he wanted. He'd be able to use that as a wedge to drive between Laura and me."

"Did you ever talk to Laura about her father's behavior?" Alice said.

Miller's hands flipped up. "Oh sure. She told me he acted that way toward every guy she ever dated. Like he was jealous. She kept telling me not to worry about it, that he'd eventually warm up to me." He snorted. "That's a laugh. You know, Laura told me that when she was a year old, they were coming home from a party. Apparently Jack was drunk, so her mother was driving. They were arguing, and her mother got distracted, ran a red light, and they were T-boned by a pickup. Laura wasn't injured very badly, and Jack only had a cut on the head—but Laura's mother died on the way to the hospital. She told me he never forgave himself for that. It's been eating at him his whole life."

"He gave up drinking?" Snow asked.

Miller shook his head. "Hell no. He got worse! She said on the weekends he'd drink himself into a stupor—until one night, when she was sixteen. She said they were sitting there watching a movie on TV, and he got up to get another drink. On the way back, he leaned over and kissed her on the forehead. Then the lips."

"What did she do?"

"She said she slapped him and jumped up out of her chair—ran up to her room. Neither one of them ever said anything about it. But after that, his drinking tapered off. Eventually he quit completely. Now he despises anyone who drinks at all. Instead of being a drunken asshole, now he's a sober one."

"Was he ever abusive towards Laura, that you know of?" Alice said.

"No. He doted on her, gave her just about anything she wanted."

"Do you think there might be any reason he would want to harm her?"

Miller flipped his hands up again. "None that I know of. I'm the one he'd like to harm."

Alice turned her head toward Snow as if deep in thought, her eyes narrowing.

"What?" Snow asked her.

She put a finger up in front of her lips and then turned her head toward the open patio doorway, listening. She got up slowly, slipping the nine-millimeter out of her shoulder holster and lowering it to her side, the muzzle pointed toward the floor.

Snow got up too, staring at her in disbelief. She glanced at him and pointed toward the screened patio doorway. He raised his hands in front of his waist, palms up.

But she was already moving quickly toward the patio door like a two-legged cat. Snow stood with his hands on his hips, watching as she reached for the handle of the sliding screen door with her left hand, her nine-millimeter moving up.

Alice threw the screen door open and moved through the opening, bringing the gun up with both hands in front of her.

"*Fuck!*" came a startled voice from behind the wall. "*Don't shoot! Don't shoot! What the fuck?*"

She lowered the gun. "Jack," she said. "What are you doing here?"

Snow recognized the man's voice now. "I just wanted to hear what that sonofabitch had to say. And it's just like I figured—trying to put the blame on me—for everything. You're supposed to be questioning him about *him*—not me! He's the suspect—not me!"

"Oh Jesus." Snow shook his head and strode toward the patio. He stepped through the doorway and stood glaring at Jack Roberts. "Roberts—I thought we agreed you'd head back to your motel and go to bed."

The man stood with big eyes, his shoulders sagging, his arms hanging at his sides. "I decided to come back," he said.

Alice holstered her handgun. "Do you realize you're trespassing? That we could get a patrol unit dispatched out here and have you arrested?"

Roberts looked from Alice to Snow and back to Alice. "I just wanted to hear what sort of lies he had to say—about me."

Snow sighed, staring at him. "Look. You didn't hire us to babysit you. That's not the sort of work we do. Now, are you going to start listening to us?"

He jabbed a finger at Snow. "You work for me—not the other way around."

"Goddammit," Snow muttered.

Alice touched Snow on the arm as she brushed past him. "Let me talk to him, Jim," she said, her voice low. "You go back inside. I'll walk Jack to his car."

"Alright," he said. Then he slipped back through the doorway, glancing at Miller. Noticing, as the man sat perfectly still, staring at Snow, that his eyes had grown larger, his complexion whiter. He looked like a corpse.

Five minutes later, Alice walked back in through the front door.

"He's on his way back to his motel," she said as she crossed into the living room. "I don't think we'll have any more trouble out of him." She sat down on the sofa next to Snow.

"What did you say to him?" Snow asked.

"He just needed to calm down," she said. "He's lost his daughter. He doesn't feel that he has anyone left. He's suffering through some anxiety."

"He ain't alone!" Miller declared.

They turned their heads toward him. He was sitting with his feet flat on the floor, his hands resting on the arms of the chair, like a man waiting to be executed.

No one spoke for a moment.

"We're going to have to ask you some questions," Snow said. "And I want you to know we're here to help you—provided you're innocent."

Miller nodded solemnly. "I know. Go ahead."

Snow pulled his notepad out of his back pocket and began. "Why don't we start with your activities on the day of the murder, Tuesday."

Miller looked down into his lap for a moment, and then up and to the left of Snow's head as though he were seeing a replay of the day's events projected onto the wall. "I was off that day. Didn't do much; went over to the park and shot some hoops for a while in the morning, then came back, did some laundry, vacuumed. I called Laura around noon. She's usually up by then, but I got her voicemail."

Snow studied his face. "You called her home phone or cell?"

Miller shifted his gaze to Snow. "Both. Why is that important?"

"I don't know that it is. It probably isn't. Later on I may find that it is. Don't worry about it; I ask a lot of what seem like impertinent questions." Snow paused, looked down at his notepad, and then back up at Miller. "Did you leave a message?"

"Yes, on her cell phone."

"Did she call you back?"

He shook his head. "No."

"So, then you...?"

Miller kept his eyes on Snow. "I sat around here, watching movies on TV until around three thirty. Tried both of her numbers again. No answer, so I headed over there to see if I could catch her at home. Got there around four and met Crystal coming out of the front door. She told me Laura wasn't home, so I left and came home. Sat around here drinking some beer and watching a couple of baseball games on TV. Had dinner around nine. Went to bed probably about ten.

"The next morning, I was making breakfast when the police showed up..." He looked down at his hands, his eyes watering. His mouth opened and closed slowly, like a fish out of water.

Snow gave him a moment. "Did you make any calls from your home phone during that time?"

Still looking at his hands, he shook his head.

"Were you on your computer at all? Anything that might show you were here?"

He looked up at Snow, his mouth hanging open. "No."

Alice leaned forward. "When you saw Crystal coming out of her front door, how did she seem to you?"

Miller cocked his head to the side and looked at the carpet in front of his chair. "Well, I must have startled her, because when

37

she saw me walking toward her, her eyes got big. She seemed in a hurry, kind of impatient and nervous."

"Does she always act that way toward you?"

Miller looked at Alice. "Yes, I'd have to say she does. She used to be friendly toward me, but after this last breakup with Laura—I think she's gotten tired of putting up with me. You know, calling all the time, showing up at the house. Can't say I blame her, really."

"What about you and Laura?" Snow asked. "I'm sure you had arguments…"

"Yeah, sure. Who doesn't?"

"Did it ever get physical?"

"Never."

"You ever hit her?"

"No."

"She ever hit you?"

"No. She had a temper, but her expressions of anger were always verbal. She liked to slam doors. That was it."

"Did you argue a lot?" Snow asked.

Miller nodded. "Quite a bit. She was a handful."

"You never had the urge to hit her, push her…anything?"

"To be honest, some of the time I wanted to strangle her. But I didn't. She knew how to piss people off."

Snow looked him in the eye. "You didn't kill her?"

Miller stared back at him. "No, I didn't."

"Who do you think did?"

Without hesitation, he said, "Tyson Dole. Laura's tenant. He and his wife rent her home in North Las Vegas. Laura was scared to death of him. He's extremely volatile—he threatened her more than once. Nothing direct—a lot of innuendoes. He's more than three months behind in the rent. Laura had started the eviction process."

"How do you know about this if you hadn't been speaking with Laura?"

Miller crossed his arms. "We talked sometimes since the breakup. Whenever she felt like talking, or—I guess—needed someone to talk to. I think that when she was scared, she felt safer talking to a guy."

CHAPTER 6

"What do you think?" Alice said.

Snow fired up the Sonata and looked over at her. "I have to say, I think Kevin Miller comes across like a straight shooter. I can understand why Mel thinks he had nothing to do with the murder. He seems innocent enough to me."

"I hate agreeing with Mel, but I was thinking the same thing. So where does that leave us?"

"Tyson Dole. He definitely goes to the top of the list. Crystal was the last to see Laura alive, but there's no motive with her. Except maybe PMS and an argument over whose turn it was to do the dishes."

Alice shook her head and rolled her eyes. "And she keeps a pair of men's size twelve work boots sitting around to disguise her tracks in case she gets the urge to drag a body out into the desert."

"And then there's Jack Roberts. No will or insurance policy on Laura. So there's no motive other than the fact that he's a perverted nutcase."

"I don't think it's good to talk that way about our client," Alice said.

"You want me to lie? I don't know why you feel the need to defend everything he does—and coddle him."

"I'm not coddling him," she argued. "I treat him with respect and try to honor his wishes because he's our client. I'm trying to run a business here, Jim. We can't handpick the people we want to work for, or we wouldn't have enough of them to make a living. I don't want to be critical of you, but you need to think about the way you treat the people who hire us. We work for them."

"Well, hell," Snow said. "Alright, I guess you're right. I'll try to be a better person from now on."

Alice laughed. "Well, don't strain yourself."

Snow chuckled. "Okay. What about phone records? I think we need to get a copy of Laura's recent cell phone activity. How do we do that?"

"Jack already has it. He started a crude investigation of his own before he decided to hire us. He called her service provider and told them she'd been murdered and he needed the information."

"And they gave it to him, no questions asked? I thought you needed something signed by a judge these days."

"He's the next of kin. She's dead. He gave them her full name, date of birth, social security number, address, city of birth. So they gave it to him. He said he'd e-mail the phone records to me when he gets back to his room."

"You think that's where he is right now?" Snow said.

Alice straightened in her seat and stared out through the windshield. "God only knows."

Silence filled the inside of the car, the two of them lost in their own thoughts.

Finally, Alice spoke.

"Jim, there's something I need to ask you."

"What's that?"

"Are we going to sit here in this driveway all night?"

"Oh, yeah," Snow mumbled. "I knew there was something I was forgetting." He shifted into reverse and backed onto the street.

CHAPTER 7

The next morning, after a ten-mile run, a shower, soft-boiled eggs, toast, and coffee, Snow picked up his phone to call the office.

Alice picked up on the first ring. "It's almost nine. What are you still doing at home?"

"Good morning, sweetheart," Snow said. "I love you too."

"Seriously."

"Seriously, this was my morning for LSD. Two cups of coffee, and I still haven't recovered from it."

"What does that stand for?"

"Long slow distance," he said, sipping coffee.

"How many miles?"

"Ten."

"Very good. So, you're really going to do it this year?"

"Just the half marathon. Not the full."

"That's still impressive. You're my hero. How long until you get here—for work?"

"It might be a little longer before I can leave. I have some things I need to do around here before I leave."

"Like what?"

"Picking out my attire for the day. I'm torn between the gray sharkskin suit with the eel-skin oxfords, or the Italian wool with the alligator loafers."

She laughed. "Sharkskin suits went out with plaid bell-bottoms. The only suit you own is the black one you bought from J. C. Penney for your mother's funeral."

Snow took another sip of coffee. "I can't wear that. If I spill my lunch on it and somebody dies, I'll be in a bind."

"I don't care what you wear, Jim, as long as it's not a T-shirt, or your pajamas, or Bermuda shorts. What time do you think you'll get here?"

"An hour. Maybe a little more. Did you have a chance to look at Laura's cell phone records?"

"I did, and I found something interesting."

"Which is?"

"A lot of calls to her dentist's cell phone. More than thirty in the two weeks leading up to Laura's death. I called the number on the statement and talked to him. He's the one who supplied the dental X-rays to the crime lab."

"That makes sense, since he was her dentist."

"Thirty phone calls in two weeks," Alice declared. "I wonder what else he was to her?"

"I'm thinking of a bad joke," Snow said.

"Drill, baby, drill?"

"You read my mind."

"Jim, it doesn't take a psychic to figure that one out. Anyway, the dentist's name is Andrew Tully, and he says he'll be home all day. I told him we'd probably stop by in the afternoon. Does that fit your schedule?"

"Perfect. I'll see you in a bit."

Snow disconnected the call and dialed another number. He didn't expect Leon Stapper, the CEO of Dep Tech, to answer. Though Snow was sure he would be in today. *Probably sitting there right now at his desk in the heart of Silicon Valley*, Snow thought. *Sifting through paperwork and e-mail messages.*

The recorded voice of his executive assistant came on the line. Snow left a message and waited.

Fifteen minutes later, Snow's phone rang. It was Leon Stapper. He sounded a little anxious. "You left me a message about Corina?"

"Who is Corina?" Snow asked.

His voice grew louder. "My daughter! You left a message saying you needed to talk to me about my daughter."

"Oh. My mistake," Snow said. "I should have been more specific. You have a daughter named Alice?"

Silence. Snow waited a few seconds. "Mr. Stapper? You have a daughter named Alice James?"

Finally he answered, his voice low. "How do you know about her? Who are you?"

"I'm Jim Snow—"

"Yes, I already know that," he snapped. "How do you know Alice?"

"She's a close friend," Snow said. "I work with her."

Stapper hesitated for a moment. "Is she alright?"

"She's fine—thriving in fact."

Stapper sighed. "I'm glad to hear that; it's been a long time. Where are you? What is she doing now—for a living?"

"Las Vegas," Snow replied. "She was a homicide detective here, a good one. Spent quite a few years on the force. We recently started a private investigation firm together."

Stapper's voice evened out—his daily business voice. "The two of you need money? Is that why you called?"

"Money is a little tight right now, as to be expected, but we're fine. That's not why I called."

Stapper said nothing.

"I called," Snow continued, "because she talks about you all the time. I just wanted you to know that it would mean a great deal to her to be able to talk to you. It's obvious that you're on her mind a lot."

"Oh…well…that's good to know. I'll have to give her a call when I get a chance."

"She's in the office right now," Snow suggested. "She's there alone; it would be the perfect time to call her. Would you like the number?"

"I'm a little busy right now," Stapper insisted. "Well, hell, I'm always busy. Why not. Go ahead—I've got a pen here."

"Now, there is one thing I'd like you to do for me, Mr. Stapper…"

"Certainly."

"Don't tell her I called you."

"How do I explain how I got her work number?"

"Oh yeah, I didn't think of that," Snow said. "Well, tell her you got the number from a private detective. Then it won't even be a lie. She can assume you hired one to find her."

CHAPTER 8

With butterflies fluttering about inside his stomach, Snow opened the front door to the suite of offices, hurried past the vacant reception area, turned right, and strode down the hallway into Alice's office.

Standing in front of her desk, he put his hands on his hips and let out a breath. "Sorry I'm late," he said.

She nodded, smiling. Stood up from her swivel chair, her fingertips lightly touching the desktop. "I just want you to know that is the nicest thing anyone has ever done for me."

Snow forced a look of mock confusion. "What are you talking about?"

"You know what I'm talking about," she said. "My father. You called him and asked him to call me."

A half grin formed on the right side of Snow's mouth. "I did not!" he protested.

She lifted her fingertips off the desk, turned slowly, and walked out from behind it—toward Snow. She stopped in front of him, her face only inches from his. She kissed him, then wrapped her arms around him and placed her head on his shoulder.

Snow felt his own arms encircling her waist, as if they had a mind of their own. And the two of them stood like that for a few moments, her warm breath on his neck.

"What did he have to say?" Snow murmured.

"He wanted to know if I needed any money," Alice replied.

"Well, that's good," Snow said. "That shows concern. A father should ask his daughter if she needs money—just to be sure. What else did you talk about?"

"He wanted to know what I had been doing since the last time he saw me, which was practically my whole life. I gave him the abridged version. He asked about my mother, how she got along after he left. I told him she met someone nice, they got married and had my two brothers. And how he turned out not to be so nice after all, when he snuck off in the middle of the night with a waitress who worked at a greasy spoon we always ate Sunday dinner at."

"Was your stepfather…was he…?"

"Yes," she said. "He was one of your people. My mother only dated white men. Even in Detroit, that was fairly unusual back then. But my mother was a looker; she had no trouble attracting them. She just couldn't hang on to them."

They moved apart. She walked back behind her desk to her chair and sat down. Snow slid back the client chair in front of her desk and plopped down. "Is your mother living alone now?"

Alice smiled. "She never married again, and she lives alone. She's still in Detroit, and my brothers and I visit her as often as possible."

"That's good. So she doesn't get lonely being by herself?"

"Definitely not," Alice said. "She has a lot of friends. She has her church activities. And she's on the Internet all the time, on those dating sites, looking for new prospects. Some guy from Florida drove all the way up there in his RV to meet her. They drove around the country in it for three months. Then he dropped her off and went back to Florida." She laughed. "One of my brothers called me and told me about that. He said Mom told him she wore him out—he had to leave because he couldn't take it anymore."

Snow chuckled. "She must be in pretty good shape."

"She goes to the gym quite a bit, plays tennis, and walks four miles a day. Strangers have approached her, asking for her autograph—they think she's Tina Turner."

"How does she handle that?"

Alice shrugged. "She gives them the autograph."

Snow grinned. "Sounds like quite a lady. So, what about you?" Snow asked. "When are you planning to see your father?"

She made a sour face and shook her head rapidly. "No way."

"No way—what? What are you talking about?"

"All these years gone by. He won't bother himself with flying out here to see me."

Snow frowned and folded his arms. "What did he say?"

Alice leaned to the side and rested her cheek on two fingertips. "He said he'd give me a call next time he comes to Vegas."

Snow unfolded his arms and spread his hands. "Well, there you go!"

"There I go *shit*," Alice said. "He's a bullshit artist. That's how he got to be CEO of a big, bloated corporation like Dep Tech. He's got no reason to want to see me."

"You're his daughter. He loves you."

She offered a pained expression. "He doesn't love me. He doesn't even know me."

"He doesn't have to know you to care about you. There's a biological bond, and that can't ever be broken."

She leaned forward in her chair. "That's one of those bonds that was made without any glue. But that's okay. I'm a grown woman; I don't need him."

Her eyes growing damp, she bit the side of her lower lip and lowered her gaze to the scattered papers on top of her desk.

Snow took in a deep breath and looked down at his shoes, letting it out slowly. He could think of nothing more to say.

CHAPTER 9

Tyson Dole was thirty years old, of medium height and build. He had blond hair, combed straight back. He opened the front door of his home with glazed eyes and a sneer on his face, his right hand firmly gripping a can of cheap beer. He shifted his gaze from Snow to Alice, then back to Snow. He gave Snow a nod. "How's it goin'?"

"Good," Snow replied. "Mind if we come in?"

Dole stepped back from the doorway, spreading his left arm out dramatically in a welcoming gesture. "Welcome to my castle," he said. Then he raised his beer can. "Cold one?"

Alice and Snow stepped inside.

"No. We're fine," Snow said. "Why don't we sit down?"

"That sounds like a plan, boss," Dole said. "How about the living room? Go ahead and seat yourselves while I replace this empty." He tipped the can to his mouth and chugged the remainder of its contents. Then he flung it toward the wastebasket, banking it off the side of the cabinet and in.

"Nice shot," Alice said. "I can tell you've been practicing."

"With diligence. I could hit that thing with my eyes closed," Dole declared on the way to the refrigerator. He swung the door open, reached inside, and brought out a fresh can of beer. Popping it open, he carried it into the living room and fell backwards into the recliner. He leaned back in it, forcing the leg rest up. With his beer can resting on his stomach, his eyes focused between his sneakers at Alice and Snow, he belched and said, "Alright—I'm in the suspect interrogation position. Fire away."

Alice and Snow looked at each other, then back at Dole.

"To start with," Snow began, "we want you know that we're on your side, and we're here to help you."

Dole's expression remained unaffected. "How so?"

"I expect that you had nothing to do with Laura Roberts's murder?"

"I'm completely innocent," Dole declared.

"Well, after we uncover evidence leading to the perpetrator, he'll be arrested, and you'll be in the clear."

Dole took a swallow of beer. "That sounds good, boss. But if you expect that I'm innocent, why are you here talking to me instead of the suspects?"

"We don't really have any suspects at this point. So we're starting out by talking to anyone who knew Laura and might be able to give us helpful information."

"And what sort of helpful information would you like me to give you?"

Snow leaned forward and spread his hands. "Is there anyone you know of who might have wanted her dead?"

In one smooth motion, Dole leaned forward, kicking the leg rest down. He gripped the beer can in both hands, his elbows resting on the arms of the recliner. His eyes narrowing, he said, "I don't like speaking ill of the deceased, but I can tell you for a fact, anyone who ever exchanged words with that woman might have wanted her dead—at least for a few minutes. Or even a few seconds."

"Why do you say that?"

"She had a knack for firing insults that could drive a comatose lobotomy patient into a rage. And it happened, at least with me, anytime she wasn't getting the answers she wanted to hear. There were times she got so bad she reminded me of that possessed girl in *The Exorcist*. But the thing is, it wasn't just the things she said. It was her expressions, her delivery, that would make you want to toss her off a bridge."

Sitting on the sofa next to Snow, Alice gave Dole a thoughtful look and crossed her legs, smoothing out her skirt with her fingers. "Sounds pretty bad," she said. "And how did you react to her?"

Lowering an eyebrow, Dole said, "Cool. I don't let people like that bother me. Just let it flow past me. It doesn't pay to lose your cool just because some asshole wants to ruin your day even worse than it already is."

"And how have your days been recently?" Alice asked.

Dole took a slug of beer, lowered the can, and crumpled it slightly, making it pop. He nodded. "Pretty fucking bad."

Alice said nothing. She waited.

He took another pull on the beer and continued. "I work construction. April and I moved down here six years ago from Sioux Falls, South Dakota. Things weren't that lucrative up there, and we heard it was booming in Vegas. It was. I was making a lot of money for a few years. But it all came to a screeching halt.

"I got laid off five months ago; some of my buddies have been out of work for a year or more." He looked down at his crumpled beer can, tilting it to examine the dents he'd caused. He sighed and continued. "One more month and my unemployment will stop coming in. Maybe they'll give me an extension and I'll get another six months. I don't know.

"But that's not enough to live on anyway." He looked up at Alice. "April, my wife, works as a cashier at the Boulder Nugget; she doesn't make much of anything. We're more than three months behind on the rent. Dead landlady won't keep us from getting evicted. I heard her old man is a worse asshole than she was." He spread his hands, the beer can in his right. "So why would I bother to kill the bitch?"

"So, what's your plan now?" Snow asked.

Dole raised his can of beer in front of himself and then lowered it. "Drink myself to death," he said. "Just like Nicolas Cage in that movie."

"*Leaving Las Vegas*," Snow said.

Dole nodded. "That's the one. I've studied it many times. That's the way to go out."

"I don't think you'll get there drinking beer," Snow advised. "It doesn't have enough alcohol in it. You'll just end up fat and dying of a heart attack at fifty."

"Well," Dole said, "I can't handle hard stuff; it makes me barf...goddammit!" He lowered his head and shook it.

"What about your wife and kids?" Alice said. "You don't care about them?"

He raised his head slightly, peering at Alice past his eyebrows. It gave him a demented appearance. "They don't need me. They're hardly ever here. The kids treat me like a stranger, and my wife is screwing her boss."

"What makes you think that?" Snow said.

"She lost fifty pounds. Wears more makeup than Tammy Faye Bakker. She looks at the guy like those fifteen-year-olds used to look at Elvis." He shook his head again. "It's pretty sad, I tell you. Before we had the kids, she used to look at *me* that way. Used to whisper sexy things in my ear. We'd sit on the couch every night—I'd be rubbing her feet, and she'd be asking me if I still loved her. Now she asks me if I farted."

Dole took a swig of beer and continued. "It's going to be tough on her, having to break it off with the guy. He's married with kids. We'll probably have to move back to Sioux Falls and stay with her parents. That'll suck for a while, and then eventually I'll be arrested for murder and spend the rest of my life in prison."

"Not if you're innocent," Snow insisted.

Dole shot Snow an evil glare. "I'm not talking about the murder of Laura Roberts. I'm talking about my mother-in-law."

Snow looked down at his hands for a moment, thinking, then back up at Dole. "Tyson, have the police been here to talk to you?"

His head tilted a bit, his eyelids beginning to droop. "Oh hell yeah. They showed up the morning after the murder. Grilling me. Searching the place. My car."

"They find anything?"

He scowled. "Hell no! I didn't do it!" He drained the rest of the beer, crumpled the can in his fist, and hurled it at the wastebasket. It missed and went skidding across the linoleum, stopping in front of the cabinet doors under the kitchen sink.

"Did they take anything with them?"

"Pair of work boots."

"What size?"

"Eleven and a half."

"Pretty old?"

"No," he said. "Practically new. I just bought them two weeks before I got laid off. Haven't had a need to wear them since then—obviously."

"Would you mind telling us where you were last Tuesday night?" Snow said.

Dole snorted and got up. He went into the kitchen, leaving the empty can on the floor, and dug another beer out of the refrigerator. After popping it open, he took a drink from it. "I'm starting to get the impression you two are homicide detectives, working for the *man*. Mind showing me your stinking badges?"

Snow interlocked his fingers and rested his arms on his thighs. "We don't have any stinking badges. We used to be cops, but not anymore." He stood up, picked a business card out from inside his wallet, walked over to Dole, and handed it to him.

Dole looked at. "This doesn't mean anything," he said. "Anybody can have business cards printed up to say whatever they want."

"If we were police officers, we would be required to tell you."

"Bullshit!" Dole snapped. "Not if you're undercover. You could come into my home and tell me any story you want." He tossed the card on the counter. "*Goddammit!*" he yelled, loudly enough to make Snow's ears ring. "*I am sick and tired of this shit!*" He threw his beer at the sink. The can bounced out and rolled across the vinyl counter, spilling a small river of beer across it.

His eyes wide, his upper lip pulled up exposing yellow teeth, he growled, "I want you two out of my house. Right now!" He jabbed a finger at Snow and then at the front door.

Snow studied the man's face for a few seconds and then let his shoulders drop. "Alright, we'll go."

He turned and walked toward the front door. Alice had risen from her seat on the couch and met him at the door. Without saying another word, they opened it and stepped outside. Walking briskly along the sidewalk, Dole yelled after them, "And don't you two assholes ever come back! You hear me? I know you think I'm guilty! But that doesn't bother me! You know why?"

At the curb, next to Snow's Sonata, they turned to take one last look at Tyson Dole, just in time to see him raise his tortured expression to the sky and bellow, "*Because I don't give a shit!*"

To Alice, Snow murmured, "Jesus. How do we defuse this situation?"

"I think we can only aggravate it further," she said. "Let's get the hell out of here before somebody calls the police."

CHAPTER 10

It was noon when Alice James and Jim Snow arrived at the Boulder Nugget Hotel and Casino. The parking lot was more than half full, an encouraging indicator in a city struggling to join the nation's tepid recovery—with unemployment nearing fifteen percent, and home prices low enough to allow an old Chevy to qualify as a down payment.

They left the Sonata parked on the second floor of the parking garage and took the stairs down to ground level. Inside the casino, the coolness of fresh oxygen pumping through the ductwork greeted them.

All around them, like nesting pigeons, Las Vegas locals sat in front of the machines. With a drink in one hand and a cigarette in the other, they stared bleary-eyed at the colorful displays, their expressions showing no more excitement than you would find in a Laundromat.

They approached the cashier's cage and asked a young Asian woman if April Dole was back there somewhere.

The cashier turned to a shapely brunette, wearing the standard white shirt and black trousers. "April!" she called to her.

April's back was facing them as she stood at the rear table, facing the wall, scribbling on a form. Hearing her name, she turned her head toward the Asian cashier.

"These people want to talk to you," the cashier told her.

April turned completely around, offered a smile to Alice and Snow, and walked toward them.

Alice offered her business card. "Is there a chance we might take a few minutes of your time?"

"Let me check," she said, and then she crossed briskly to an open doorway that led to a back room. She came back through the doorway a minute later, holding Alice's card with both hands, and forced a smile. "I'll meet you over at the Starbucks," she said. "Do you know where that is?"

They nodded and left.

A few minutes later, sitting at one of the small tables, Alice and Snow saw her striding purposefully toward them, holding onto the purse strap that was draped over her shoulder as though someone might suddenly lunge at it from behind a slot machine. They stood and introduced themselves, shook hands, and sat back down.

"We don't want to take up too much of your time," Alice began. "So we'll get through this as quickly as we can."

April nodded and smiled. "It's not a problem," she said.

"We understand you and your husband have had some problems with your landlady Laura Roberts."

She straightened in her chair. "More like she had problems with us. My husband and I had to stop paying the rent. He's been out of work. We're more than three months behind. She told us she would be starting the eviction process." She shrugged. "That's to be expected."

"You never argued with her about it?"

"I didn't," she said. "But Tyson got pretty worked up with her a few times. She was always coming over to the house trying to get money out of us—money we just didn't have."

"How did she come across?"

"Rude, inconsiderate, belligerent—hostile."

"Did she make you angry?"

April's eyes widened. "Oh yeah!"

"How did you react toward her?"

She shrugged. "I just walked away and let Tyson deal with her. I didn't want to talk to her. I don't like dealing with people like that."

"And Tyson? How did he usually react?"

She shook her head slowly, frowning. "Like he does with just about everyone who pisses him off: yelling, name-calling, swearing."

"Did he ever threaten her?" Snow asked.

"No. He doesn't threaten people. Just yells, swears, and throws things—but not *at* anyone. He's all bark and no bite."

"Is there any chance that he might have tried to harm her?" Snow said.

April shook her head. "No. That's not like him. He doesn't even like to spank the kids. He makes me do it."

Snow nodded. "Were you home with him Tuesday night?"

She looked down at the table, her face flushing. "No. He was home alone. I didn't get home until around five in the morning. I had the kids with me."

Alice and Snow glanced at each other, then back at April.

"Do you mind if we ask where you were?" Alice asked.

She swallowed, pressing her lips firmly together. She continued to stare at the table without answering.

"Tyson thinks you're having an affair with your boss," Alice said. "Is that who you were with?"

She let out a short laugh and looked up at Alice. "No. That's silly. My boss is a nice guy. We're good friends. He has a family. I've never been involved with him. Tyson has an overactive imagination."

"Who were you with?" Alice pressed.

April sighed. "Okay, there has been someone else. He stopped me for speeding. He's a police officer—works for North Las Vegas. He's a really nice guy. I gave him my cell phone number. He called me, and it developed from there." She shrugged. "It was one of those things. I wasn't looking for an affair—it just happened."

Alice and Snow said nothing.

"He's wonderful," April continued. "He picks the kids up from school for me sometimes and takes them to his place. They adore him. I spent the evening there with him Tuesday night."

"So no one can vouch for Tyson's whereabouts Tuesday night," Snow said.

She shrugged and nodded. "That's true, unfortunately. But I'm sure he was home all night. He couldn't have gone anywhere for very long."

"What brings you to that conclusion?" Alice said.

"Because I took the garbage out before I left for work Tuesday morning. When I got home Wednesday morning, there must have been at least twenty empty beer cans in there."

Snow shifted his eyes toward Alice and raised an eyebrow. He leaned forward, pulled his notepad out of his back pocket, and scribbled.

Alice looked at his notation, rolled her eyes, and shook her head. To April, she said, "How many beers does Tyson drink in an hour?"

"Two, on average," she said.

"And what time does he usually start drinking?"

"Around nine o'clock in the morning."

"So," Alice suggested, "if he drank from nine a.m. until three p.m., that would be twelve beers. Then even if he got back as late as nine p.m., he could have easily finished off eight more beers by one a.m."

"That's true," April said. "I guess empty beer cans isn't much of an alibi."

"No, it's not," Alice agreed. "It suggests that he was sitting around drinking and brooding, and possibly got himself worked up into a frenzy—and acted on impulse."

Snow scribbled some more, then looked up at April. "How are you dealing with all of this?"

April folded her arms. "This has been pretty bad. Worse than anything I've ever been through in my entire life. I've tried to get Tyson to see a counselor, but he has always refused. I know there aren't any jobs around here, but I suggested to him that he could drive a truck. They always need long-haul truckers, and the pay isn't that bad. He'd have to live in a truck practically all the time. And sleep in it, and eat at those truck stops. But it wouldn't be that bad. A lot of people do it. But he didn't like that idea.

"And now all of this is going on with the murder of our landlady. The police have been interrogating both Tyson and me, and some of our friends; now you're here. Everybody's been looking at me funny, and I know they're talking behind my back about it.

"Anyway, Donald and I have talked about this, and he wants me to move in with him right away. I think that's best; in fact, I know it's best. I need a clean break from this situation. So I've decided to notify Tyson that it's over, and I'll be coming by the house to pick up some clothes and stuff as soon as I get off work this afternoon."

Alice leaned forward, her eyes narrowed. "Notify him—how?"

Her teeth clenched, April let out a breath through her nose. "Text message," she said. "As soon as I'm finished here with you, I'll send it. There's no sense putting it off any longer. I can't take any more." She jabbed a finger toward Snow. "And I'll suggest Tyson not be there when we show up because I'll be bringing Donald along with me—and he'll have his gun with him—just in case."

CHAPTER 11

"What do you think?" Alice said.

"The chili macaroni is fantastic. Just the right amount of tomato sauce; the spice factor has been pushed to the limit without going overboard. This is what I like about this buffet—they serve a lot of different home-style dishes. You won't find dishes like these at many of the other buffets. Stuffed peppers, cabbage rolls, chicken livers, casseroles—it's almost like a potluck." Snow shoveled another scoop of chili macaroni into his mouth and grinned, chewing happily.

"It amazes me that you don't weight four hundred pounds, the way you eat."

"It's all the running and weight lifting," Snow said. "Burns a lot of calories. Did you know your muscles burn calories while you're sleeping?"

"So that's what's been keeping me up those nights I can't sleep. Anyway, I meant about the case," Alice said. "What are your thoughts on the investigation? And why are you using a soup spoon to eat that with?"

Snow finished chewing and swallowed. "It's the only utensil that works. You try to load this stuff onto a fork, and it'll all fall off on the way to your mouth." He took a sip of lemonade. "I know what you're thinking: I don't have any manners. I used proper etiquette most of my life. Now that I'm older and smarter, I do what makes sense."

"What would you do if the Queen of England were sitting here with us?"

"I'd ask her if she was lost." Snow glanced at Alice's plate. "I can't believe you're not interested in the collard greens. It's usually pretty salty, but not so much today. And there's a lot of meat in it. They're very tasty."

"I can't stand collard greens," Alice said, working her knife through a section of sliced turkey breast.

Snow switched to his fork and stabbed a few green beans with it. "That's hard to believe, considering your heritage," he said.

"I'm not from the South," she said. "I'm a Yankee."

"I thought collard greens were a universal staple of your people." He put the forkful of green beans into his mouth and munched thoughtfully on them.

"I was never made aware of that," Alice said. "And you may have noticed I'm not that partial to fried chicken, ribs, or watermelon either."

He pointed his fork at her. "Now that's downright un-American."

Alice impaled a small piece of turkey with her fork and aimed it toward her mouth. "I like hot dogs, burgers, and pizza. I also like lutefisk. Isn't that considered a traditional favorite of *your* people?"

Snow wrinkled his nose. "That stuff is terrible. I was forced to eat it nearly every Sunday when I was growing up. My mother's parents loved it. Every time we went to visit them, they'd make it. It was like mush."

"I adore it," Alice said. "But you have to prepare it properly. I'll have you over for dinner one night and make it for you. I think you'll like my version of it."

He shook his head. "I doubt it, but I'll give it a try. I like to keep an open mind. If it isn't any good, we can always order a pizza."

Alice giggled. "You really know how to please a woman."

From his front jeans pocket, Snow's phone chirped. He set his fork on his plate, pulled the phone out, and flipped it open. He looked at the display and muttered, "This guy always calls when we're eating."

He put the phone to his ear. "Jack, what's up?"

"Just checking in," Jack said.

"Okay," Snow said. "Thanks for calling."

"Anything?"

"Not yet," Snow said. "We'll be in touch." He snapped the phone shut and put it in his pocket.

"You don't think that was a little bit rude?" Alice asked.

Snow took a sip from his glass of lemonade and set it back down.

Before he could comment, the phone in Alice's purse began to ring.

Arching his eyebrows, Snow said, "Now you get your chance."

"It's not him," she said, reaching into her purse. "It's probably a prospective client. Think positive."

She checked the number, pressed the talk button, and placed the phone next to her ear. Smiling, she tilted her head and chimed, "Hello, Jack. How are you today?" She looked at Snow, rolling her eyes. "Actually, I'm sitting here with Jim as we speak, so I can't tell you anything more than he did, okay?...I know...I know...Sometimes we do split up if we have a lot of ground to cover..." She rolled her eyes again. "Okay, Jack. You have a good day. Try not to worry. I know this is tough for you, but try to occupy your mind with a pleasant distraction for a while if you can. Maybe see a movie or something...Okay, sure...You're welcome...Bye-bye." She disconnected the call.

"If you expect me to start talking to him like that," Snow muttered, "I'll have to start wearing pink underwear."

She dropped the phone into her purse and resumed eating. "I can't believe he called both of us."

"He likes to cover all of his bases—limited as they may be."

"Anyway," Alice said, "back to my original question..."

Snow ate some more green beans, thinking. Finally, he said, "I don't know. Obviously we have to continue on with the Tyson Dole angle. We can't eliminate him. After lunch, we talk to the dentist, see where that takes us. After we finish with him, we could talk to Dole's neighbors, see if any of them saw him coming or going Tuesday night. What do you think?"

Alice nodded. "Sounds good."

Snow put his fork down and crossed his arms. "You know what I was thinking, Alice?"

"What's that?"

"I think you should take the initiative. Make the first move."

She screwed up her face. "With Tyson Dole?"

"No. Your father. Leon Stapper. Call him and invite him out for a weekend. Tell him you'd like him to stay at your home so the two of you can get to know each other."

"Are you crazy?" Alice protested. "Someone like him? He's rich. Why would he want to stay with me? He probably books a penthouse at the Bellagio when he comes here."

"Well," Snow insisted, "you offer, just to be gracious, but let him stay where he wants."

"And I expect he has a young, blonde-haired, blue-eyed girlfriend he would want to bring along. He might feel a little uncomfortable introducing her to a forty-one-year-old black woman—as his long-lost daughter. Imagine the look on her face."

"Definitely a Kodak moment," Snow said.

They laughed.

And continued to eat in silence, each lost in their own thoughts.

CHAPTER 12

Andrew Tully owned a two-story home located in what appeared to be a ten- to fifteen-year-old development off East Summerlin Parkway, a couple miles east of Highway 215. His residence was a three-bedroom, with a manicured front lawn and palm trees on both sides.

He answered his doorbell promptly, offered a nervous smile and a clammy handshake, and then invited Alice and Snow inside. They seated themselves at one end of the leather sectional sofa, while Tully assigned himself to the opposite end.

Wearing a yellow polo shirt, black pleated slacks, and penny loafers, Andrew Tully appeared to be in his late twenties or early thirties. A slight fellow of average height, his short brown hair was parted along the side, with the front hanging down over his forehead at an angle. He was attempting to project an air of well-being and self-control, but failing at it. His eyes were dark and puffy, his complexion pasty, his movements jerky—and his entire body seemed to quiver.

Putting his hands together in his lap, he settled his gaze on Snow. "Can I get you some coffee, or perhaps a cocktail?"

Snow looked at Alice. She arched her eyebrows and shrugged. He turned back to Tully. "Whatever you're having will be fine with me."

"I'm feeling in the mood for a gin and tonic," Tully said. "But if you'd like something else, I have a full bar…"

"That sounds good to me," Snow said. "I haven't had one of those in a long time."

Tully looked at Alice.

"Count me in," she said.

He got up and left Alice and Snow to gaze about the living room, taking in the various paintings covering the walls.

"Nice taste," Alice said.

"Yeah. Nice variety. A few forest, mountain, and lake scenes. We've got the ocean, some animals, and a flower."

Alice narrowed her eyes. "It makes me wonder why he isn't married. A dentist with a beautiful home, expensive furniture, and paintings. Probably a Mercedes in the garage."

Snow was studying the painting of the flower. "It's possible he's gay," he suggested.

"You aren't partial to flowers? I bet a lot of men can appreciate the beauty of a flower," Alice said.

"Maybe, if it's sticking out of a cactus," Snow suggested.

"Or a woman's cleavage?" Alice countered, giving him a look.

Tully appeared from behind the wall leading into the family room, carrying a tray of drinks. He set the tray on the coffee table and handed them out.

After seating himself at the end of the sectional sofa, Tully took a swallow, crossed his legs, and rested the glass on his knee. "This has been a rough week for me," he said, gazing at his cocktail.

Alice took a sip of her drink and placed it on a wooden coaster on the coffee table. "Business is good then, I take it," she said.

"Not really. It's actually been pretty slow for the last few years, but I've only been practicing as a dentist for a little over four, so I'm still trying to acquire new patients. And it's tough right now because very few people in Las Vegas seem to have money for routine exams and cleaning. They wait until they're in pain, or crack a tooth, or their gums are swollen and bleeding. Some of the people who come into my office haven't seen a dentist in five to ten years."

Alice winced. "That's awful."

"It is horrible," Tully agreed. "I feel sorry for these people. But it's tough on me too, because I'm not making much money, and I'm dealing with one emergency after another. It's rare that anyone makes an appointment ahead of time, and when they do come in and I get a look inside their mouths, I feel like I need to call in a wrecking crew to deal with it."

"I'm curious," Snow said, "why you chose Las Vegas to establish your practice."

"I love the desert," Tully said, appearing to warm to the conversation. "Especially Las Vegas. I had considered Phoenix, but it's too big, and it doesn't have the glitz of this city. I'm originally from San Francisco..."

Snow nodded and nudged Alice with his elbow.

Tully took a sip of his drink and continued. "And I love that city, but it's very expensive, and it would be extremely difficult to set up a practice there without a lot of money."

"Your parents...?" Alice asked.

"My parents have money, but I wanted to get started on my own without their financial help. I mean, they put me through school, of course, but once that was over, I wanted to start the next chapter with a feeling of independence and self-reliance."

"That's admirable," Alice said.

"Plus, I was exiting a bad relationship, and I felt I needed a clean break and a fresh start in a new city. It was very difficult because we were engaged to be married, and she and I had been together since we were twelve."

Alice nodded and nudged Snow. "Not to pry, Andrew, but I'm surprised you haven't met anyone else here in Las Vegas."

His face twisted into a lopsided grin. "Actually, I have. And we're engaged."

"Congratulations. Is she...one of your patients?"

"Yes, in fact, that's how I met her. I don't go out much, and I'm not comfortable with Internet dating sites."

"Give my best wishes to your fiancée," Snow said. "And on the subject of patients, we understand you provided the dental X-rays to the police to identify the remains of Laura Roberts."

Tully's face lost more color. "Yes, that was a hard thing for me. That's what I was referring to when I mentioned this being a rough week."

"Of course," Snow agreed. "Also we noticed a lot of phone calls to you from Laura on her cell phone record during the last couple weeks before her death. Naturally, we're curious about that since we're investigating her murder."

Tully's mouth dropped open. "Her phone record. How did you manage to get her phone records? I thought you had to have a subpoena or something."

"Oh, we got them legally, not to worry about that. Was Laura a friend, or maybe she had a lot of questions about her teeth?"

Tully frowned and took a swallow of his drink. "The truth is we were close friends. I had known her for years. She was to be the maid of honor at our...our...wedding. I'm engaged to her best friend."

Alice thought about this for a moment, a frown forming on her face. She stared at Tully. "Who are you engaged to?"

"Crystal Olson. We've planned for a May wedding."

Snow drew his eyebrows together. "Okay," he said. "Crystal and Laura were roommates, so that would mean you saw a lot of Laura, probably just about every time you went over to their house. You must have gotten to know her very well. I expect there were a lot of nights with the three of you sitting around watching TV together, maybe double-dating now and then. What you're telling us is that you developed a relationship with Laura. Platonic of course. But good friends, nonetheless." He raised his eyebrows. "Is that right?"

Tully nodded. "Most definitely. Laura was very friendly and easy to talk to. We shared a lot of our problems. I've always felt it's easier to open up to women about personal issues. You know, with guys it's just a lot of joking around, talking sports—nothing very deep."

"I see," Snow said. "And this friendly exchange went on for how long?"

"About a year," he said. "For as long as I've been involved with Crystal."

"The thing I'm wondering about, Andrew, is that it looks like the vast majority of the calls from Laura to your cell phone—and vice versa—only occurred within the two weeks leading up to her murder. Before that there were hardly any. Why is that?"

Tully sat perfectly still, staring hard at Snow with big eyes. He resembled a mime staring at a car wreck. Nothing came out of his mouth. No words. Not even his breath.

"Andrew?" Snow pressed.

Suddenly he flinched and started breathing again. He rubbed his chin with his fingertips. "A few weeks ago," he began, "Crystal and I started having problems with our relationship. There were a number of disagreements between us that escalated into heated arguments. It got so bad that Crystal even called off the wedding." He took a sip from his drink and continued. "I was devastated, of course, and confided in Laura. I had tried everything to repair the rift between us: apologies, Hallmark cards, flowers, foot massage, an expensive necklace. Nothing worked. I was desperate. I called Laura and asked for advice. And we continued on, calling back and forth, in an attempt to try and salvage the wedding plans." He blinked several times and smiled with the lower half of his face.

Snow stared at him for a moment and then shifted his eyes toward Alice. "Anything more you want to ask, Alice?"

Alice met Snow's gaze. "Nothing I can think of at the moment. I think we've pretty much covered everything for now."

CHAPTER 13

Snow parked the Sonata a half block down the street from Tyson Dole's residence. The two of them split up, canvassing the neighbors. Alice took the house across the street from Dole, the home next to it on the west side, and Dole's immediate neighbor on that same side. Snow covered the homes on the east side.

No one answered across the street, but an elderly woman greeted Snow in the house next to Dole. She was short and plump with curly gray hair. Her smile spread from ear to ear, her eyes swimming behind the lenses of her thick, rimless glasses. "What can I do for you?" she chimed.

Snow offered his business card. "We're investigating a homicide, and I was wondering if I might come in for a few minutes to see if there's anything you might know that would be helpful to us."

Her smile faded. "Who got killed?" she asked.

"May I come in?" Snow said.

The woman stared at his face as though reading a tea leaf. "Oh, sure, sure, come in. I'm sorry, my head's not on straight." She stepped out of the way and allowed Snow to pass in front of her.

"Why don't we go into the dining room. I've got some fresh iced tea. And the boys are in there playing cards. They might know something I don't—although I doubt it. They don't know much of anything these days."

Snow followed her through the living room into the dining room, where he noticed two identical, white-haired old men sitting across from each other at the table. They were both completely bald on top, with matching haircuts, and gold-rimmed glasses. They appeared to be playing blackjack, both of them with several uneven stacks of multicolored plastic chips. The only feature that distinguished them apart was a two-inch scar below the left eye of the one with the most chips. They seemed oblivious to Snow and the old woman.

The one with the scar had split aces in front of him, and the other twin dealt a card for each face down. Scar-face lifted both cards and flipped one over. It was another ace. "Split 'em again," he said.

"You can't. You only get one split with aces."

"Bullcrap," scar-face said. "You said we were playing Boulder Highway rules, Donnie."

"The hell I did. I said we were playing downtown rules."

"No, you didn't. And even if you did, the rules are different downtown. It depends on the casino."

"What's the main drag in a downtown, Dennis? Main Street. We're playing Main Street Casino rules—no re-splitting aces."

"Boys," the old woman interjected. "We've got company."

They both turned their heads toward Snow, their faces wrinkled in matching frowns.

"What's he selling?" scar-face asked, staring at Snow. "He looks like a vacuum cleaner salesman. I already bought one of those fancy vacuums forty years ago. Cost me a fortune and wasn't much better than a Hoover."

"He's not selling anything," the woman insisted. "He's a homicide detective—somebody got killed."

"Who? Who got killed?" scar-face asked.

"Dennis, you sound like an owl," the other twin observed.

Scar-face slid his chair back from the table, stood up, and ambled over to Snow, offering his hand. "I'm Dennis Ball, Detective. This is my wife Darla." He motioned toward his twin, sitting at the table. "And that's my brother Donnie. He lives across the street. But he's always here."

"I'm Jim Snow, but I'm not a homicide detective," Snow said, letting go of Dennis's hand. "I'm a private detective."

"No kidding," Dennis said. "I've never met one before. How did you get into that line of work?"

"I spent a lot of years with Metro as a homicide detective. Got tired of it, so my partner and I thought we'd give it a try."

"And how do you like it?"

Snow shrugged. "It's like anything you think you might want to do for a living—once you start doing it, it begins to suck."

Dennis grinned and nodded. He waved a hand in the direction of his brother. "Donnie and I decided to start our own plumbing company—forty-four years ago. Seven days a week we worked. Middle of the night we'd get calls and have to go out. Frozen pipes, sewers backed up...all kinds of stuff. Once we got the business going, we couldn't get out of it. What else we gonna do for money, right? You can't just shut it down and go to college. Where would the money come from for that?"

"Ah, Dennis, it wasn't that bad," Donnie countered. "There are worse jobs."

Dennis gave him a dismissing wave and put his hands on his hips. "Well, sure there are, but you're missing the point, you pinhead. I'm just trying to add to the conversation here."

"So am I," Donnie insisted. "You just always want everybody to shut up so you can do all the talking."

"Boys," Darla said. "Let's not do this in front of company."

"What company?" Dennis said. "He's a homicide detective. He could care less—"

"He's a private dick," Donny corrected. "He just told us that. Look who's calling the kettle stupid."

Dennis shook his head and looked at Snow. "Can you imagine working with that yokel for forty-four years? Darla and I moved down here to try and get away from him, and what's he do? He buys the house across the street from us. He's over here every morning before breakfast, starting it up."

Darla pointed a finger at her husband. "And you love every minute of it. You can't wait for him to get here. If he isn't over by seven, you traipse over there to get him up."

"He's old," Dennis said. "I've got to make sure he's not dead."

Snow chuckled. "Where are you from?"

"Huebner, Minnesota," Donnie announced. "And I don't miss it one bit."

"I miss the loons," Darla said.

"I don't understand why," Donnie said. "You married one." He slapped himself on the thigh and cackled.

She gave them both a dismissing wave and headed into the kitchen.

"I grew up in Abbott," Snow said.

Dennis arched his eyebrows. "I'll be damned. That's, what, twenty miles from Huebner?"

Snow grinned and nodded.

Donnie's expression perked up. "You spend much time at Deebs Lake?"

"Oh yeah," Snow said. "We were there most weekends in the summer. We had a pop-up camper, and that was the old man's favorite destination."

"We pulled a lot of walleyes out of that lake," Donnie said.

"No, you're thinking of Osakis," Dennis said. "All we ever caught at Deebs Lake were sunfish and a few bass."

"You never caught any, but I did," Donnie insisted.

"I don't remember that."

"You were asleep."

Darla came back carrying a tray with four iced tea glasses. "Why don't you two quit lying." She set the glasses on the table and the tray next to them. "I swear, they're like kids. Every time we have company, they start acting up like they're on a talk show or something."

"He's not company," Donnie said. "He's a private dick. And he's about to tell us who got killed."

Darla put her hand on Snow's arm and gave him a gentle shove toward the chair at the end of the table. "Why don't you sit down, Jim, and drink your iced tea."

He thanked her and sat down. Darla picked up a glass and seated herself at the far end across from Snow.

Snow picked up his glass of iced tea and took a sip, noticing three sets of eyes trained on him, waiting.

He set the glass down. "Laura Roberts," he said.

Dennis and Donnie looked at each other.

Darla's hands went to her cheeks. "Oh, my Lord, no," she said. "She was just a young thing. How did it happen?"

"Somebody hit her in the head with a baseball bat," Snow said.

Darla's hands remained on her cheeks, as if her face might explode. "Oh, that's terrible! Who would do such a thing?"

Dennis turned his eyes to Snow. "Just about anyone who ever met her," he declared.

"Is she the cocktail waitress who owns the house next door?" Donnie asked.

Turning to his brother, Dennis said, "Yeah, that was her. She was easy on the eyes, but hard on the ears."

"Dennis!" Darla snapped. "Would you have some respect for the deceased?"

"Just stating the truth," he mumbled, then took a drink of his iced tea.

"Do you have any idea who did it?" Darla asked.

"There hasn't been any evidence uncovered yet that would point to anyone."

Darla clasped her hands together and put them in her lap. "I wonder if it was a home invasion. I always worry about that."

Out of the side of his mouth to his wife, Dennis said, "Nobody in their right mind would invade our home, Darla. What would they get? Our stereo is a ghetto blaster, the computer runs on DOS, and the television we bought back when Ronald Reagan was president."

"Nothing was stolen," Snow said. He paused, thinking for a moment. "I take it the police haven't been here to talk to you?"

Darla shook her head. "If they had, we'd have known about the murder."

"That's true," Snow said.

"But now that I think about it," Darla said, "I'm pretty sure there were some detectives talking to Tyson Dole, next door. There was an unmarked car with those government license plates parked in front of his house, and then a van showed up. They were there inside his house for quite a while. I just thought it was related to Tyson's usual crazy behavior."

"Was that Wednesday?"

"Yes, I believe it was. So she was killed Tuesday evening? Tyson's not a suspect, is he?"

"Had they found anything," Snow said, "they would have taken him into custody. And yes, she was murdered Tuesday evening. The body was transported out to an isolated section near Red Rock Canyon, and it was set on fire to destroy any evidence there might have been."

Dennis piped up. "Tyson Dole didn't kill that woman."

Snow looked at him. "Why do you say that?"

"I'm pretty sure he was home all night. Tuesday night we had meatloaf." He turned his eyes to his wife. "Right, Darla?"

"Yeah," Donnie agreed. "That's right. Tuesday night was meatloaf. Wednesday was chicken and dumplings."

"I guess that's right," Darla added.

"I remember that night," Dennis said, "because my memory of it is attached to the meatloaf. That's how my mind works. And after dinner, from about six thirty until almost nine, we were out on the patio. We could hear him over there yelling and cussing like he always does."

"That's right," Darla agreed. "That was Tuesday night, and I remember the racket coming from over there."

"Do you know who he was yelling at?" Snow said. "You think there was somebody over there with him?"

"He might have been on the phone," Dennis offered. "People are always on the phone these days. Darla and I were in the checkout line at Albertson's once, and the woman behind us started yelling like crazy. I thought she was yelling at us, but we turned around and she was on the phone, yelling at some-body else."

"I think he might have been watching a baseball game," Donnie said. "I've heard him yelling at the TV."

"Sometimes when it's not even on," Dennis added. "He's crazier than all get out."

"I think it's that house," Darla said. "I think it's possessed. Just like that Amityville house where that doctor lived."

Dennis gave her a scowl. "There wasn't a doctor living there. You're thinking of James Brolin, who played the guy in the movie. He was a doctor on *Marcus Welby*."

"I know that," she snapped. "That's what I meant. But I'll tell you something about that house next door." She raised her arm and pointed in the direction of it. "Since I've been living here, every person who has ever been in that house has done a lot of yelling and cursing—and screaming. They don't even have to go in the house. They could be standing in front of an open doorway, and the spirit will enter their body."

Donnie nodded. "That's true. I never heard anyone yelling out in the front yard, unless they came storming out of the house first."

Snow narrowed his eyes. To Darla, he said, "Before Tyson and his family moved in there, Laura and her former boyfriend, Kevin Miller, were living there. Is that right?"

"That's correct," Darla replied. "He was living there with her for a couple of years—and they fought like cats and dogs the entire time. You know, when it's pleasant outside like it's been the last week or so, all the windows are open. Their voices carry so well, it sounds like they're in the next room."

"Did Kevin Miller ever hit her? That you know of?"

Darla shook her head. "I never saw a bruise on that girl. Or on him either."

"What did they fight about?" Snow asked.

"Whatever wasn't sitting well with her at the time, I imagine."

Snow stared at her, thinking for a moment. "You say that everyone who lived there was loud and verbally abusive?"

Darla nodded. "That's right. And before Laura and Kevin Miller, when it was Laura living there alone, she used to get into it with Crystal."

"Crystal Olson."

She nodded. "Crystal was over there a lot. She and Laura have been friends for years."

"What did she and Crystal argue about?" Snow asked.

Darla raised her eyebrows and shrugged. "Like I say, that house is possessed by something evil."

"The only thing evil in that house," Dennis mumbled, "was Laura Roberts."

Darla rolled her eyes and shook her head.

Snow suddenly remembered the conversation with April Dole. She'd be coming by with her boyfriend pretty soon. He glanced at his watch. It was five thirty p.m. "Do you know if Tyson Dole is over there now—next door?"

"No, he's gone," Donnie said. "He went tearing out of there about an hour ago."

Darla looked at the clock on the wall behind Snow. "Oh. Where'd the time go? I need to get started with dinner. Do you mind, Jim? Do you have any more questions? If you do—or even if you don't—we'd like to have you stay for dinner if you don't have plans."

Snow smiled. "Well, I don't know if I can. My partner is working the other side…"

"We've got plenty for both of you," Darla insisted. "I always make way too much."

"And tonight," Donnie said, "will be a real treat. You being from Minnesota. You're gonna love it. Tell him what we're having tonight, Darla."

She beamed. "My specialty: lutefisk."

CHAPTER 14

"What did you find out? Anything?" Snow accelerated away from the curb and glanced over at Alice.

"The first doorbell I rang, the woman took one look at me and shut the door in my face."

"What was that all about?"

"I have no idea. The house next to it, I was greeted cordially by the mother of a nine-year-old girl. Her daughter has been practicing since she was six to become a concert pianist. I was invited in immediately and entertained with fifteen minutes of classical music, accompanied by their dog singing along."

"Was she any good?"

"The girl or the dog?"

"Either one."

"The girl was pretty good," Alice said. "The dog wasn't intended to make it an ensemble. They couldn't get her to shut up, so they put her in the backyard. Anyway, when the performance concluded, I asked the woman if she had noticed whether Tyson Dole was home at all Tuesday night, and she didn't know.

"I had better luck at the house next to the Dole house. The man I talked to who lives there said he and his wife and kids could hear Tyson over there all night Tuesday night, hollering and banging things around, off and on, from the middle of the afternoon until ten o'clock."

"Didn't that bother them?" Snow asked, turning onto the main thoroughfare.

"He said they're used to it. He told me that if they know he's home and it's quiet over there, they get nervous."

"They've never called the police?"

"He told me the racket always stops by ten o'clock. And it never sounds like anyone is being hurt. What did you find out?"

"Same thing, pretty much," Snow said. "The neighbors I talked to said it stopped around nine. But that's when they went to bed. At any rate, Crystal Olson discovered the disturbed furniture at eight thirty, so that puts Tyson Dole out of the picture."

"Thank God," Alice said. "I wouldn't want to have to go into that house again."

"The people I talked to say it's possessed. That's why Tyson Dole acts the way he does. And before the Doles lived there, everybody who set foot in there had it out with Laura Roberts—including Kevin Miller and Crystal Olson."

"That's interesting," Alice said. She turned to Snow and gave him a broad smile. "You want to hear something else interesting?"

"What's that?"

"I got a call on my cell phone while I was talking to Tyson's neighbor. And you'll never guess who it was from."

"You're right," Snow said. "I'll never guess."

"My half sister. My father's daughter. Her name is Corina, and she's a doctor in San Jose, California. She's thirty-six, still single. She told me my father invited her to lunch today and told her everything about me, my mother, everything.

"I asked her if he told her that I'm a woman of color, and she said yes. She's excited to find out she has a half sister. I mean, she really sounded happy about it. She wants to come down here and meet me this weekend. I invited her to stay at my house—and she thought that would be great. We can stay up and talk all night if we want."

Snow chuckled. "That's great news. Didn't I tell you? What about Leon?"

She touched him on the leg with her fingertips. "She said she tried to talk him into coming with her, but he's leaving on travel tomorrow. He'll be in Asia for two weeks. But she said he'd like to fly down here and see me as soon as possible after he gets back."

Snow glanced over at Alice. Her face was aglow. "That's fantastic. Didn't I tell you?"

"Yes, you did. I guess I shouldn't be so cynical. And thank you again for calling my father." She kissed him on the cheek.

"This calls for a celebration," Snow said. "Someplace special."

"As long as it's not a buffet." Alice grinned.

"Or lutefisk," Snow added. He told her about the dinner invitation.

She laughed.

"Well," Snow said. "How about we swing by Silvey's Steakhouse. We can usually get in there on a Saturday night without a reservation."

"That sounds nice," Alice said. "And after that?"

"After that, I think we need to pay another visit to Kevin Miller. I've thought of more questions to ask him."

Alice nodded. "I was thinking the same thing."

"Is he out there?" The words spilled out of Kevin Miller's mouth in a thin rasp.

He stood in the open doorway to his home, like a zombie, his color gone, his eyes appearing to have sunken deeper into his skull. Gripped firmly in his right hand, the barrel pointed at the floor, was a pump-action shotgun.

"No," Snow said. "Is Jack Roberts still bothering you?"

"He's getting worse," Miller said. "He's getting enjoyment out of watching me suffer with dread before he finally kills me. I'm certain of it."

Alice and Snow stepped inside. Miller rushed to the door, shut it, and threw the deadbolt.

"I think you're overreacting," Snow said. "If he wanted to do anything that stupid, he'd have done it by now. He's nowhere around now. Has he been back here?"

"Off and on," Miller said. "He sits out there staring at the house for a while; he leaves, comes back."

They made their way into the living room and sat down. Snow noticed the sliding glass patio door was shut and locked, the blinds drawn across it. The room was warm and stuffy.

Miller leaned the shotgun against the recliner, walked over to the stuffed chair across from Alice and Snow, and sat down. He swallowed and wet his lips, his eyes wide and staring. "I went out to the garage to get in my truck to go to the store this morning around nine. I opened the garage door, and he was parked right behind it in my driveway. Scared the shit out of me. I walked over to him and asked what he wanted. He just stared at me with that sick grin on his face. Then he made a gesture of a gun with his forefinger and thumb, and pointed it at me. I asked him if that was supposed to be a threat. He didn't say a word. Just started his car and drove away slowly, staring at me. I considered calling the police, but I don't think that would do any good. They won't arrest him until he's killed me."

"He's just trying to scare you into doing something incriminating," Snow said.

"Incriminating?" Miller snapped. "I haven't done anything wrong."

"He thinks you have," Snow said. He nodded at the shotgun. "Where'd you get that?"

"A friend of mine dropped it off. I thought it would ease my mind, but it just scares the shit out of me. I don't like guns. I've never had one, never shot one, never even touched one until now. I just look at it and it gives me the jitters. I really don't think I could ever shoot anybody with it if I had to."

Snow nodded. "I know how you feel. I've never been that crazy about guns myself."

"You don't carry one?" Miller asked.

"I've asked him to," Alice insisted.

Snow shrugged. "I honestly can't remember where I put it. I hid it somewhere one night after a party. I didn't want some kid wandering around my house someday, finding it, and shooting himself with it."

"When was the last time there was a kid in your house?" Alice asked.

Snow turned his head to her. "You never know, Alice. Someday I may invite the neighborhood over for a barbeque."

Miller's eyes wandered back to the shotgun. "I've been thinking. Maybe it would be a good idea to hire someone to watch my house from the street." He turned back to Snow. "Could I hire you to put somebody on that?"

"We don't have any extra people," Snow said. "It's the just the two of us, and we're both tied up with this investigation. But I could recommend someone. When would you want him to start?"

Miller's eyebrows shot up. "Right now would be good."

"I tell you what." Snow leaned back and dug into his front jeans pocket for his cell phone. He pulled it out and flipped it open. "I can call someone right now and check to see if he's available." He looked at Miller, and Miller nodded.

He brought up a number from the directory and pressed the call button.

Two rings and a deep voice came through the receiver. "Duke Ellis."

"Duke," Snow said. "How goes it?"

"It's been worse," Duke said. "That you, Jimbo? Didn't recognize your number. Long time no hear."

"It's been a while," Snow said.

"How's the poker business? You back in it, or doing something else?"

"Something else."

"Anything fun?"

"Same thing you're doing," Snow said.

"Oh shit. You poor bastard."

"Tell me about it," Snow said. "But I do have a partner, which helps."

"Misery loves company," Ellis said. "Who is he? Anybody I know?"

"He's a *she*. Alice James. She was in homicide."

"Never met her. Sounds like a nice setup. Ironic as it may sound, I've got a new female partner, too. Sent me her résumé.

She'd been working for a national outfit, doing investigations, and wanted to get out on her own. I wasn't looking for a partner, but I get tired of having to call around to find somebody to relieve me on surveillance. Plus, I figured she'd help bring in more female-type business. That hasn't happened yet, but we've only been working together for three months. Her name is Sally Hollister, and she's the smartest, cutest little thing."

Snow grinned. "She moved in with you yet?"

"You know me too well, Jimbo. We're talking about it." Ellis chuckled. "I traded my van in on a pickup camper. We use that for surveillance. We can both be there and trade off the watch."

"You got good shocks on that thing?" Snow asked.

Ellis laughed. "Those days are over. I'm pushing sixty. I'm to the point where I view the female anatomy as an art form. But enough about me. What about you? The two of you keeping busy?"

"Not really," Snow said. "You?"

"No. It's slow. I've got a few lawyers feeding us scraps their regular guys are too busy to handle, along with the occasional walk-in client. But it's not enough to pay the bills. I've been supplementing my income counting cards on the side."

"I figured you would have been barred from the whole town by now."

"Naw, I'm careful about it. Never play for more than an hour at each casino. Never bet more than a hundred per hand. Work it from twenty-five up to that when the deck's good—but do it slow and easy, so it looks natural. And I bought a fake Rolex so I'll look like a high roller."

"Why don't you just do that full time?" Snow said.

"It's torture," Ellis said. "I couldn't sit there staring at those cards, keeping the count in my aging brain, and maintaining the act forty hours a week, fifty-two weeks a year. And I'd end up like everybody else: barred and out on the street."

"Speaking of 'out on the street,' I've got a job for you, if you've got the time right now."

"We're just sitting here watching the idiot box. What have you got?"

Snow explained the situation with Jack Roberts, and Miller's need for someone to watch his house.

"We can be over there in a half hour. Tell him it's sixty-five an hour, and if that's okay, we'll saddle up and head over."

Snow repeated the message to Miller; Miller nodded. Snow gave Ellis the okay and ended the call.

He turned to Miller. "Now we have some questions for you."

"Sure. No problem. I'm happy to help."

"Yesterday when we talked to you, you told us you and Laura fought quite a bit."

Miller tipped his head to the side and shrugged. "Yeah."

"And you said it never got physical."

"That's right."

"What about Laura and Crystal? How did they get along?"

"They were best friends."

"That doesn't tell me much," Snow said.

"They had an occasional tiff while I was around. Can't speak for the times I wasn't."

"When you and Laura were a couple, I imagine you were with the two of them quite a bit. Is that right?"

Miller nodded.

"How bad did it get between them?" Snow asked.

Miller looked down at his tennis shoes, then back up at Snow. "It got fairly heated a few times."

"What was the worst? What happened that time?"

Miller let out a sigh. "I came over one night about five months ago. Laura and I had recently gotten back together. The four of us were watching movies on TV and drinking."

"The four of you?" Snow said.

"Laura and I, Andrew Tully and Crystal. We didn't get far into the evening before Andrew and Crystal started arguing. Andrew left in a huff. Then Laura and Crystal got into it."

"What were they arguing about?"

"It was about Andrew and Crystal—I don't remember specifically—something insignificant. Laura thought Crystal was being too hard on Andrew, and that was what started them off on each other. It escalated. They began trading insults. Crystal got up from the couch and walked over to Laura. Laura stood up. And Crystal punched her in the jaw with her fist. They grabbed hold of each other and fell on the floor, rolling around and pulling hair. I got up and ran over to them. Managed to pull Crystal off from Laura; she's not very big, but she's strong. I managed to get between them and keep them apart until I could get Laura outside and get her to cool off. I didn't think it was a good idea for Laura to go back in there. So I went in and got her purse, and we drove to the Strip and went to a club."

"It sounds like both of them were hot-headed."

"Yes. But Laura was a lot different than Crystal. Laura had a methodical way of digging at people and getting them worked up. She was kind of mean that way. Crystal just reacts. Suddenly blows up and goes bananas for a few minutes and then calms down. Like a tornado passing through."

Snow turned his eyes to Alice. She met his gaze and raised her eyebrows.

Turning to Miller, she asked, "How well do you know Crystal's fiancé?"

"Not that well," he said. "I think she started dating Andrew about a year ago. The four of us got together quite a bit until Laura and I broke up the first time."

"How long ago was that?" Alice asked.

"Eight months ago. So there were only a few months where we'd hang out together. Andrew and I never really hit it off. You know how it is—the two women are best friends, so Andrew and I get dragged into the picture. He always seemed like a nice enough guy—but he's a dentist. We had trouble finding common ground. I can't even imagine what would drive someone to want to work in people's mouths all day—unless your patients were all supermodels."

Snow grinned and nodded.

"Do you know how close the friendship was between Laura and Andrew?" Alice asked.

Miller's eyes widened. "Laura and Andrew? I couldn't say. I expect no different than my relationship to Crystal. Just friends by association."

"Close friends?" Alice asked.

Miller's head jerked back as though he'd been pushed. "I wouldn't know. Not that I noticed. You mean intimate…?"

Snow cleared his throat. "Andrew told us he confided in Laura frequently regarding his relationship with Crystal. They talked on the phone quite a bit recently."

Blinking several times, Miller looked down at the coffee table, then back at Snow. "I don't know anything about that. It's news to me. You think they were having an affair?"

"I don't know," Snow said. "We were just wondering about that. It's probably nothing."

"Probably," Miller agreed. Then he lowered his eyes to the carpet and stared at it as though it were covered in blood.

CHAPTER 15

It was a few minutes past ten p.m., Saturday night. Coffee at Denny's on Boulder Highway.

Jim Snow was returning from the men's room to find Alice on the phone. She was staring into her cup of green tea, frowning.

Snow pulled his chair out from the table and sat down. He took a sip of coffee. It wasn't bad.

She looked up at Snow, her eyebrows drawn together. "You think it'll be on the news?" she said into the phone. She rolled her eyes and shook her head. "Yeah, no doubt. Hey, Mel, while I have you on the phone, you mind if I ask you something?"

Snow cocked his head and raised an eyebrow. "You're talking to Mel?"

She nodded. "Mel, did the CSAs find any evidence of the body being dragged to the front door or into the garage?" She nodded. "Okay. Thanks, Mel. We'll talk to you later." She pressed the disconnect button and dropped the phone into her purse.

She looked at Snow. "Tyson Dole has been arrested."

Snow's mouth fell open. "No way."

"It's not what you think," she said.

His eyes narrowed. "What's the charge?"

"Quite a few of them, actually. But not what you're thinking. He was running naked down Las Vegas Boulevard, between the cars, shouting obscenities and making indecent gestures to the tourists on the sidewalk. He was northbound in front of the Mirage when he was apprehended."

"Mel Harris called to tell you that? Why?"

"Because he thought it was funny," Alice replied. "He's surfing the Net as we speak, looking for video clips."

Lowering his head, Snow rubbed his forehead with his fingertips. "Well, we shouldn't be surprised. With everything he's been through, he was bound to crack."

"Too bad he's a resident," Alice said. "If he were a tourist, they'd probably just send him back to his room in the morning."

Snow put his arms on the table and looked out the window into the parking lot. "Actually, might have been a pretty smart move; now he'll get free psychiatric face time from the county. Some sort of counseling program."

"Didn't people used to do that sort of thing in the seventies—for fun?"

Snow nodded. "It was called 'streaking.' I don't think the police even took it seriously back then. There were naked people running around all over the place."

Alice sighed. "Maybe I'll make some phone calls on Tyson's behalf. Tell them what I know about him."

"That he's nuts?"

She smiled. "Yeah, I guess they don't need my help figuring that out." She took a sip of her tea and brought her eyes back to Snow. "So, what are your thoughts at his point?"

Snow leaned back in his chair, took a slug of coffee, and swallowed it. "To start with, regarding Laura Roberts, it looks like everyone agrees she enjoyed pissing people off. So, anyone who was in Las Vegas without an alibi Tuesday night could be a suspect. Tyson Dole apparently was home entertaining himself, so he's off the list.

"Jack Roberts. Another nutcase. Although he doesn't seem to me like a killer, and there's no evident motive. Kevin Miller is still a strong contender. No alibi; he had motive, means, and opportunity. He might have had a key to the front door."

"I was thinking," Alice added, "that maybe something was going on between the dentist and Laura that he found out about—and went over there to confront her."

"But they were already broken up. He would have to expect that she was seeing someone. I wonder if she was dating anyone recently."

"What about the dentist? What's his name?"

"Andrew Tully," Snow said.

"He seemed really nervous, like he knows or suspects something that he's not willing to divulge. I'd like to know what those phone calls were about. He's engaged to Crystal. Maybe he got into a sticky situation with Laura, and she threatened to tell Crystal about it. Maybe he killed her to keep her quiet."

Snow nodded and then shook his head slowly. "I don't know. That seems like a long shot."

"I don't think so," Alice countered. "We need to find out where he was Tuesday night. We didn't even ask him."

"I would have," Snow said. "But I wasn't thinking of him as a suspect. Now that I think about it—you could be right. So we put Andrew Tully on the list as a slight possible."

"Who else?" Alice asked.

Snow shrugged. "What about Crystal Olson?"

"I'd put her up near the top of the list," Alice said. "She was the last person to see the victim alive—plus she discovered the body."

"Motive isn't clear, but she already slugged her with her fist. There's a slim chance she could have graduated to a baseball bat if her temper is as bad as it sounds—and something flipped her over the edge. But what about the boots? I doubt there would be a pair of men's size twelve work boots in a house with two women."

"That's definitely a large fly in the ointment," Alice said. "No getting around that. And Crystal is a tiny woman. She'd have to drag the body out to her car."

"Or Laura's car. It was in the garage. Out of view of the neighbors and passing motorists."

Alice nodded. "She could drag the body out to the garage. But she'd have a tough time getting it into the trunk or the back seat. I don't think she's strong enough."

"She could have done it," Snow said. "But she would have scraped some skin off on the edge of the trunk. I don't think she would even try to get her into the back seat by herself. She would have to lift her torso to get it up onto the seat, and then go around to the other side and drag her the rest of the way in. That would have left some skin behind in the back seat. But the lab didn't find anything."

"So, if they used Laura's car to dispose of the body, it had to be a big, strong man, or two or more people. They didn't find any trace evidence in Crystal's car. So, somebody else's vehicle was used to transport the body. And why didn't the perpetrator just leave the body where it lay, burn the house down, and leave? Seems kind of stupid going to the trouble of taking the body all the way out to the edge of the desert and increasing the risk of getting caught."

Snow considered this for a moment. "You're right. Setting the house on fire would be a lot easier. Less chance of leaving evidence behind." He shook his head. "What did Mel say about the possibility of the body being dragged? They find anything?"

"Nothing. He said the garage floor was clean, no dust to leave a trail in. And nothing inside the house or on the front walkway."

"Maybe she swept it afterward," Snow offered.

"She would have had a busy night," Alice said. "So, what have we accomplished during our first thirty hours into this case?"

Snow considered this for a moment.

"We've pissed off our client to no end. And we helped send a deranged man running bare-assed into the streets of Las Vegas."

Alice smiled. "Now aren't you glad you gave up poker?"

Snow nodded. "It's good to screw up something different for a change."

CHAPTER 16

She came to her front door in a red tank top and scanty black running shorts. In her early thirties, she was tall and slender, with even features and straight brown hair resting on her tanned shoulders.

Alice offered a smile. "You're Erin Potter?"

The woman returned the smile. "Yes. And you're the private detectives."

Alice introduced herself and Snow, and then they followed Erin into her living room, where they seated themselves, Snow in a recliner, Alice in a flowered easy chair.

"Are you a runner?" Snow asked.

Erin hooked her lower leg under her and plopped onto the couch. She rested her hand over the bare toes sticking out from under her thigh. With a devilish grin on her face, she looked Snow up and down. "No, I just like to dress like one. It's comfortable. I'll bet you're a runner though."

Snow smiled. "How did you know?"

"You look like you're in pretty good shape. Pretty buff, too. You must work out."

Snow nodded. "I have a weight machine and a rack of dumbbells in a spare bedroom. You?"

"I wasn't born this way. Yeah I work out with weights a little. Do some elliptical, stair climber, stationary bike—whatever's available."

"Well, you look pretty good," Snow said.

"So do you," Erin said. "Tall, handsome brute like you. I'll bet you've got the women fawning all over you."

Snow chuckled. "If they are, I haven't noticed any."

"Yeah, I bet you're watching for them though. Aren't you?"

Snow's smile faded. He raised an eyebrow and stared at her. He tried to think of a clever comeback, but nothing intelligent struck him, so he remained silent.

Erin sighed and turned her head to Alice. "Have you been making much progress with the case so far, Alice?"

"It's still early," Alice said.

"I guess that means no," Erin said.

"That's a pretty good guess," Snow said.

Erin looked at him without speaking. It was an indifferent look—one she might use while peering into a sink full of dirty dishes. She turned her eyes back to Alice and smiled. "I'll do whatever I can to help you, Alice. I miss Laura. Her death was horrific news. I hope you find the sick bastard who did that to her."

"I hope so too," Alice said. "But it takes a lot of legwork and interviews with anyone who might have been in contact with her recently. We never know when a lead will pop up out of nowhere. That's why it's important that you tell us everything you know about Laura, her friends, family. Where she might have been, what she might have done that might have led to her demise. We have a standard set of questions that we usually ask, but if something pops into your mind that you think we should know—don't hesitate to tell us. Okay?"

Erin nodded. "Of course, Alice," she said. "I'll do my best." She smiled warmly.

Alice crossed her legs and started. "I take it you knew Laura fairly well?"

"We were best friends," Erin said. "I've known her for over three years. Since I started working at Shillington's; she was already there. We usually worked the same shift, four to midnight, so we hung out together a lot.

"I loved Laura right from the start. She had a lot of personality and charisma. A lot of fire. And she wasn't afraid to do or say whatever she felt like. She had guts. And I have to say, I haven't met many people like her."

"How well do you know Crystal Olson?"

"Very well. Crystal and I are best friends also. I never saw as much of her as I did Laura because she usually works a different shift. But a lot of times the three of us would hang out together. Crystal is different than Laura. She doesn't always talk much, keeps things bottled up inside her. But she's a really sweet girl, and I love her for that."

"How is her temperament?"

"Crystal? She's got one. But no worse than mine or anyone else's." Her eyes narrowed. "Why do you ask?"

"We were told she and Laura fought quite a bit, that it got physical at least once."

Erin turned her head slightly, peering at Alice out of the corner of her eye. "I hardly ever saw them arguing. They got along great. We all did. Physical in what way?"

"We were told Crystal punched Laura in the jaw."

Erin's mouth opened. She glared at Alice. "No way. I never heard about anything like that from Laura—or Crystal. And we never kept anything from each other. Who told you about that?"

"I'd prefer not to say," Alice replied. "I'm sure you understand."

Erin leaned forward. "Kevin Miller. It was him, right? You can't believe anything that jerk says. He lies about everything. In fact, he's the one who hit Laura. Eight months ago. That was the main reason they broke up. She said something he didn't like, and he backhanded her. Shortly after that, they got back together, and he pushed her so hard she fell and hit her head. That was the reason they broke up the second time."

Alice gave Snow a quick look out of the corner of her eye. Returning her gaze to Erin, she said, "Laura was involved with him for two years. That was the first time he struck her?"

"The first I know of. But who knows."

"That's quite a while."

"There could have been other times that I didn't know about. This time there was a bruise on the side of her face she couldn't cover up. She had to tell me about it. Besides, it takes some men a long time to show their true colors. Obviously, he'd been holding his frustrations inside until they came boiling to the surface."

"What sort of frustrations?" Alice said.

Erin began moving her hands in front of herself for emphasis. "Kevin Miller is a control freak. Laura Roberts was a free spirit. She refused to be controlled."

"Controlled in what way?"

"Told what she could do with her free time, where she could go, and who with. He wanted marriage and kids. She wasn't interested in that yet."

"The time he hit her—what led up to it? Do you know?"

Her face began to flush. She waved her hands some more. "Laura and I went out for drinks after work one night. We ended up here and had a few more. She was clearly too far gone to drive home, so she sent Kevin a text message saying she'd spend the night here. A half hour later, he called. He'd been asleep and woke up, realized she wasn't home yet, and called her. He didn't want her spending the night anywhere but in his bed, so he offered to come and pick her up. It was already three in the morning. She refused. They argued, and she hung up and turned off her phone. When she got home later that morning, he started in on her again. They argued. He smacked her."

"Erin," Snow said, "a lot of people hit each other with their hands. Sometimes they throw things. But that's nothing close to the violence required to kill someone. Do you think Kevin Miller is capable of hitting someone in the head with a baseball bat?"

Keeping her eyes on Alice, Erin took a deep breath and let it out slowly. "I have no doubt that he killed Laura. He finally realized he could never have her again—so he gave up and knocked her head into the next world. Maybe he regretted it after he did it. But I imagine for an instant, he must have enjoyed it."

"Okay," Alice said. "Shifting gears here, we'd like to ask you about Andrew Tully. How would you describe his relationship with Laura?"

Erin's face wrinkled into a deep frown. "Andrew and Laura? They had no relationship. Andrew is engaged to Crystal. They're getting married in May."

"We know that," Alice said. "But we've taken a look at Laura's recent cell phone record, and we noticed that Andrew and Laura made quite a few calls to each other leading right up until Laura's death. Since Andrew is engaged to Crystal, doesn't that seem strange to you?"

Erin's eyes widened. Her tongue moved out between her lips, stayed there for a second, and then moved back in. "I don't know anything about that," she said. "You'll have to ask Andrew."

"We did," Snow said. "He told us he and Crystal were having problems. That he was confiding in Laura."

Erin turned her head toward Snow. Glaring at him, she said, "Well, there's your answer."

"More than thirty phone calls in a two-week period," Snow said. "That's a lot of confiding."

She stared hard at Snow. "So you believe men and women who aren't dating, or married, only call each other when they're interested in an illicit fuck."

Snow thought about that for a moment. With a hangdog look on his face, he cleared his throat and looked at Alice. "You have any more questions for Ms. Potter, Alice?"

Alice grinned at him. "I think that about covers it for now."

Outside Erin Potter's front door, on the way to the car, Alice chuckled and turned her head to Snow. "You sure you don't know that woman from somewhere, Jim?"

"Positive," Snow said. "Jesus, she acts like she's one of my ex-wives. I don't understand where the animosity was coming from. She was all over *you*."

"Maybe she picked up some bad vibes you were putting out."

"What bad vibes?" Snow said. "I was nice and friendly, like I always am. She must not like the way I look—or something. The goddamn bitch. If we have to come back here for more questions, I think I'll stay in the car."

CHAPTER 17

Duke Ellis's rig was parked on the far side of the street, across from Kevin Miller's driveway. It consisted of a white Dodge pickup with dual-wheel rear tires and a truck camper of the same color, with a window looking out over the roof of the cab.

There was no one in the truck. The curtains on the front window of the camper were open halfway, but the window was so darkly tinted Snow couldn't see inside. He parked the Sonata in Miller's driveway, and he and Alice got out.

Snow could make out an exchange of mumbling coming through the open windows and roof vent. The rig began to bounce around on the truck springs, followed by the sound of a small door opening on the far side of the camper.

A tall, slender man with weathered features, a bushy gray mustache, and a straw cowboy hat emerged from behind the rear corner of the camper. Following close behind was a short woman with silver hair, cut short. They both wore blue jeans, Western shirts, and cowboy boots.

Starting across the street with Alice beside him, Snow grinned at the couple. "Duke. You're looking good, man."

Ellis stood with his hands on his hips. "So are you, Jimbo," he said. "Looks like your hair is growing back. You been using that Rogaine stuff, or did you join the Hair Club?"

"Neither," Snow replied. "I think you've been staring at the sun too much. It's affected your vision."

"Nah," Ellis said. "Only when there's an eclipse." He emitted a coarse laugh.

Snow walked up to him and gripped his hand, slapping him on the shoulder.

Ellis motioned toward the silver-haired woman. "This is Sally Hollister, my associate, main squeeze, and harshest critic."

Sally smiled. Introductions were made all around.

Then Snow stepped back and looked at the camper. "This is nice. You just use this for spying on people, or you take it out on the road?"

Ellis lifted his straw hat and scratched his head. "Oh yeah, this is a multipurpose rig. Every chance we get, we take it out and go exploring." He screwed his hat back down. "In fact, when we retire in a few years, we plan on living in it for a year, maybe longer. Sell the house and live cheap. You ever heard of Slab City?"

Snow shook his head.

"It's an abandoned World War II Marine base in the middle of the desert in southern California. They tore everything down, and all that's left are the cement slabs. It's huge. There are about a hundred and fifty hardened souls living there year-round, through the heat and all. But when it cools off in late fall, thousands of snowbirds head down there and live for free. They get their prescriptions filled on the other side of the border. There's a river nearby with fish in it. They even have a homemade golf course."

Snow raised his eyebrows and nodded at the camper. "That little thing won't be big enough for that. You'll need a fifth wheel."

"Nah, it'll be fine. All we need is something to sleep in. During the day, we'll be hiking, fishing, golfing, or just sitting in our lawn chairs looking at the mountains."

Alice was staring at the camper. "Does it have a bathroom?" she said.

"Sure does, honey," Sally said. "Five-gallon bucket." She burst out laughing.

Ellis chuckled. "No, it's got everything you'd find in an apartment—just a lot smaller. You want the tour?"

They went inside.

Ellis was demonstrating how the dinette turned into a bed when the sound of a car approaching grew louder. They could hear it ease to a stop in front of Miller's house, the drone of the V-8 idling.

Stepping toward the side window, Ellis spread two slats of the blinds with his fingers and peered through. "It's Roberts again," he whispered.

"What's he doing?" Snow asked.

"Just sitting there, looking at the house."

Snow came over to the window and peeked out. "Does he know you're watching the house?" he whispered.

"I don't think so. We've always been inside the camper when he shows up."

"How often does he come by?"

"It varies. Sometimes hours will go by. Then he'll drive by every fifteen minutes for a while."

"Obsessive-compulsive," Snow said.

"Nuttier than a fruitcake."

"Jesus," Snow whispered. "Now we'll have to stay in here until he leaves."

"Want to play some checkers?" Ellis asked.

"Twenty bucks a game?"

"Fifty."

"Let's do it," Snow said.

CHAPTER 18

"What the hell has been going on out there?" He stood in the open doorway, his face looking like a thinner version of the clown from Jack in the Box. Holding his shotgun at his side, Kevin Miller was livid.

"I've been losing my ass," Snow muttered.

He and Alice came in, went to the living room, and sat down. Snow noticed the patio door was wide open, letting in the warm September air through the screen. *Must be feeling more secure with the Duke Ellis team guarding the house,* Snow thought. That was a positive sign.

"He was out there again," Miller said. "I saw him drive up from the upstairs window. I saw your car pull into my driveway, so I came downstairs. But you never came to the door. So I went back upstairs to see what happened to you, and you were gone. Then Jack drove up, so I ran back down here and got my shotgun ready."

"We were inside the camper," Alice said. "When Jack drove up, we had to stay in there until he left."

"What were you doing in Duke's camper?"

"Checking his surveillance equipment," Snow said.

"Have you been getting enough sleep?" Alice asked Miller.

"More than I was before," he said. "It's a comfort to me to know there are two experienced detectives guarding my house twenty-four hours a day. But I forgot to ask them—they *are* armed, aren't they?"

"At all times," Alice said. "Both of them."

"But I didn't see any sidearms when they were here. Where do they keep their guns?"

"Ankle holsters, I expect," Alice said. "It's not a good idea to have your weapon exposed. It can alarm people."

"Tyson Dole can testify to that," Snow muttered.

Alice gave Snow a look, shook her head, and rolled her eyes.

"Testify to what?" Miller asked. "What's going on with Tyson Dole?"

"Nothing," Alice said. "We've investigated him. His neighbors verified that he was home the night of the murder. We've eliminated him as a suspect."

"Who does that leave?" he asked.

Alice interlaced her fingers and placed her hands in her lap. "A lot of people," she replied. "Probably some we don't even know about yet."

"Then this could go on for some time."

Alice nodded. "It could."

"And who's on the rotisserie today? Me?"

Alice shifted her gaze to the coffee table, gathering her thoughts. Then she brought it back up to Miller, her expression unaffected. "Kevin, we talked to Erin Potter, and she told us she wasn't aware of any fight between Crystal and Laura. That Crystal never struck Laura—but that you did."

Miller's eyes lit up. "That's bullshit. She's lying. She's a lying bitch."

"Why would she lie about that?"

Miller shrugged. "Because that's what she does. Who knows what her reasons are? Maybe she's protecting Crystal or someone else. Maybe Laura lied to Erin. I know she doesn't like me—she may be lying to cause trouble for me."

"Why doesn't she like you?"

"I think mainly because I'm a man. Another reason may be jealousy."

"Jealousy? Why?"

"Because she wanted Laura and couldn't get her."

"But they were close friends."

"Erin wanted more—she's a lesbian."

Alice considered that. "What gives you that idea?"

"I don't believe she's ever had a date with a guy her entire life."

"Is there someone she's involved with now?"

"I don't think she's had a steady girlfriend. She has a lot of issues. I get the impression she must have been overloaded with sexual abuse as a kid. Now she hates men. I could be wrong, but that's the feeling I get."

Snow leaned forward, folded his hands together, and rested his elbows on his knees. He appeared to be speaking into an imaginary microphone. "You and Laura broke up the first time eight months ago?"

"That's right," Miller said.

"What caused that breakup?"

Miller spread his hands. "A lot of things. I wanted marriage and children. Laura just wanted to have fun. She would never agree to marriage. In fact, our relationship got to the point where she was no longer interested in me."

"What makes you think that?"

"She told me. She said she was only with me until she could find somebody else. She told me she knew I wasn't the one for her, and if I wanted to leave I could. Otherwise she would only stay with me until the right guy came along."

"And you were okay with that situation?"

"I had two choices," Miller said. "I could stay, or I could leave. If I left, there was no hope for me. If I stayed, she might change her mind about me, and the situation could improve."

"What caused you to leave, finally?"

"Laura, Crystal, and Erin had a girls' night out together. Apparently they got back to Erin's house and continued to party. Laura was too drunk to drive, so she sent me a text message saying she would be spending the night. I had been asleep. I woke up to an empty bed, got up to check my messages, and found her text message. She had only sent it a half hour earlier, so I called her and offered to pick her up. She said she would spend the night there."

"And the reason," Alice interjected, "that you didn't want her spending the night…?"

Miller arched his eyebrows. "I didn't want Erin Potter putting the make on my girlfriend."

"What about Crystal?" Snow asked. "Was she also spending the night?"

Miller shrugged and shook his head. "I don't know. I imagine so."

Snow raised an eyebrow, imagining the scenario. It was an attractive image. "So what happened after that?"

"She came home the next morning—or I should say later that morning—and we argued about it. She told me she wanted me out of her house. So I left."

"During the argument you never struck her?" Alice said.

"I didn't even touch her," Miller insisted. "I've never hit anyone, ever, in my entire life. You can ask anyone who has known me."

"There was a time when you pushed her? When she hit her head?" Alice said.

Miller shook his head. "Nothing like that ever happened."

"After all that—why did you want her back?"

"I loved her. I always have."

"Even though to her you were nothing more than a stand-in?"

"That may sound stupid and pitiful to you," Miller said, his eyes beginning to dampen. "But I always hoped I would someday graduate to something more in her life. If I just gave up and walked away for good—I would never have that chance."

"She must have been something terrific in bed," Snow said, backing out of the driveway.

Alice wrinkled her face up at him. "You men are all alike. All you think about is sex."

Shifting the Sonata into drive, Snow gave a wave to the camper and accelerated down the street. "In the teen years," he said, "I would have to say that's true. But as we mature, we begin to appreciate some of the finer things in life."

"Like beer and food," Alice suggested.

"And sporting events," Snow said. "We must have something to watch while ingesting the beer and food."

"What about *Dancing with the Stars*?"

Snow moaned. "Good God. If I were a woman, I think I'd kill myself."

Alice chuckled softly.

"At any rate," Snow said, "what do we do now? We've got Kevin Miller on the rotisserie, as he said. Should we continue down that road, or what?"

"We don't have anything concrete yet," Alice said. "We have Erin's word against Kevin's. That won't get us anywhere. We need to talk to more people." She reached behind her and pulled a flat black case up off the floor of the back seat. She set it on her lap, unzipped it, and removed a twelve-inch notebook computer from the case. After removing a mobile broadband connect card from the pocket of the case, she plugged it into a USB port and booted up the computer.

"What are you searching for?" Snow said.

"I'm wondering whether Kevin Miller has an ex-wife somewhere. We could talk to his family and friends. But I'm fairly sure they would be reluctant to say anything negative about him. You never know. But I was thinking it might be better to start with a negative viewpoint and work our way up—if we have to."

Snow nodded. "Good thinking. I like the way your mind works."

CHAPTER 19

They were sitting in Alice's office, Alice at her desk in her swivel chair, Snow beside her in his chair. The speakerphone was positioned between them on the desk.

The woman's voice came through the speaker a little tinny, yet clear. "Hello, this is Deanna."

Alice leaned toward the speakerphone. "Hello, Deanna. This is Alice James, and I have with me my associate, Jim Snow."

Snow leaned forward. "Hello, Deanna. I want to thank you for taking the time to talk to us. We know how valuable Sundays can be, and we want you know how much we appreciate your willingness to help us."

"Oh, it's no problem," Deanna said. "I wasn't doing anything spectacular. The kids are with their grandparents, and my husband is still at the golf course. I've just been catching up on some reading."

"Your parents live there in Kansas City near you?" Alice said.

"Yes, they're only a few miles away, so it's convenient for us. They come and pick them up a couple weekends a month and entertain them. It gives Clinton and me a chance to relax for a while and have some time to ourselves."

"You're from Kansas City originally?" Snow asked.

"Yes."

"And how about Kevin Miller?"

"Yes," she said. "Kevin and I grew up together. We went to the same schools. He was the first boy I ever dated, and we went steady all through high school and got married when we were nineteen."

"That's fairly young," Alice said. "I imagine it must have been difficult being married at that age."

"It was," she agreed. "We weren't making much money. Kevin was working at a grocery store, stocking shelves; I was a receptionist. We ended up living with my parents after my daughter was born, which was a year later. We didn't move out on our own until we were twenty-two. Kevin was able to get on with the fire department here in Kansas City around that time, and I started making a little more money."

"I take it you moved to Las Vegas with Kevin?" Alice asked.

"Yes, that was a few years later. We were twenty-five. We had both Emily and Megan." She sighed. "I really didn't want to leave Kansas City. All of my family is here. But Kevin was excited about it. It was all he talked about. I mean, I also had serious reservations about the move because Las Vegas is...well, it's 'Sin City.' With all the gambling and prostitution—what kind of a place is that to raise kids?

"But after we got there and got settled in and bought a house in Henderson, it wasn't so bad. I mean, after you get away from the Strip, it's like any other city. It has a lot of parks, and the schools were nice. I even got used to the heat."

"It's really only hot for three or four months," Snow said.

"That's true," Alice chimed in. "Then it drops down to ninety-five."

Deanna giggled. "Yeah, that's true. For sure."

"How long did you live here in Las Vegas?" Alice said.

"A little over three years. Kevin and I started having problems shortly after we got there. But it wasn't the move. I can't blame it on that. Although, I was missing my family."

"What do you think caused it?" Alice asked.

"Oh," she sighed. "I don't know. I started having doubts, I guess. I mean, I never dated anyone but Kevin. I started to wonder if I was married to the right guy. How can you know for sure, when you've only been involved with that one person your whole life?

"Don't get me wrong. Kevin is a really nice guy. He was a family man to the core. Cared about his kids and me. He always did the right thing and hardly ever complained about anything."

"He sounds like a great guy," Alice said.

"He is," Deanna said. "But he's kind of wimpy. He doesn't have any backbone—kind of like a wet dishrag. He does whatever he's expected to do, whether he likes it or not. He wouldn't stand up for himself, or me, or the kids. Never.

"I hate to say it, but Kevin is sort of a coward. And that was the biggest problem for me to deal with. I finally realized I didn't want to spend the rest of my life married to a chicken. I needed a rooster."

"That's too bad," Alice said.

"Well, not really. I mean, all in all, it worked out pretty well for us. There was no anger or fighting during the separation or the divorce. I realized later that Kevin probably wasn't that happy being married to me either. I think we started dating out of convenience. We just somehow came together; we were in the same place at the same time."

"How did he react when you told him you wanted a divorce?"

"He didn't get mad or anything. He was pretty calm. He just said okay and asked if I wanted him to move out right away. I told him to take his time and find a place to live he would be happy with. But that I would be filing for the divorce the next day. He just said okay. And that he was sorry he hadn't lived up to my expectations."

"He never tried to convince you to get back together with him?" Alice said.

"No. He signed the papers. He was very generous—always has been."

"He's paying child support?"

"Yes. He pays it on time every month. Calls the kids every month or so, and at Thanksgiving and Christmas."

"Did he ever show hostility toward you?" Snow said.

"No, never. Kevin was always the perfect gentleman."

"He never struck you?"

"Never. He's not that sort of person."

"Never pushed you?"

"No."

"It sounds like he may have kept his frustrations bottled up inside. Do you think that's the case?"

"No," Deanna said. She sighed. "With Kevin, I think it's a case of not enough testosterone. I don't know how else to put it. There's just no fire inside of him. I don't think the pilot light is even lit."

"Is it possible," Snow said, "that there's a side of Kevin you didn't see? Is there any chance that he could have gone off the deep end and lost his temper and his sense of judgment long enough to kill someone, perhaps?"

"No," she said. "I've known him nearly all of his life. There's just no way that's possible. Not for a guy like him. Believe me."

"Alright," Alice said. She looked at Snow and raised her eyebrows.

Snow shook his head.

"I want to thank you, Deanna, for taking the time to talk to us."

"You said this was in regards to a murder that happened there...is Kevin a suspect?"

"Probably not," Alice said. "We're just talking to as many people as we can. We're not really sure what we're looking for or what we'll find. This is a tough case."

"This woman who was killed—was she someone Kevin knew very well?"

"She was a former girlfriend of Kevin's. He'd been trying to get back together with her for quite a while."

"He must have cared a great deal for her," Deanna said.

"Yes," Alice said. "Apparently he did."

"But she didn't care for him."

"Apparently not," Alice said.

There was silence for a moment.

Her voice was lower, barely audible. "That's too bad."

Alice and Snow leaned closer to the speaker. To Snow it sounded like she was weeping.

"Are you alright, Deanna?" Alice asked.

She sniffed. "Yes, I'm okay. It's just a little sad."

"What's that, Deanna?"

She sniffled softly for a moment. "Well...Kevin never cheated on me. Never. That's something that wasn't in him. I never respected that, I guess. Never thought about it until recently."

"I see," Alice said.

"The thing is...I told you my husband was playing golf..."

"Yes."

"I know he's not playing golf. He took his clubs and shoes and his balls—but he's not playing golf." She sighed and sniffed. "I wanted to marry a rooster. And I finally did. But I think I married one who likes to chase all the chickens around."

CHAPTER 20

Shillington's Hotel and Casino was located on Flamingo Road, west of I-15 and a little over a mile west of the Palms. The casino was a rectangular building, surrounded by a series of arched entryways and fancy columns, giving the impression the customers were on their way to visit royalty.

The gambling floor was constructed with high ceilings, multiple hanging chandeliers, and various carvings that looked as though they belonged on the prows of great sailing ships. The carpet was decorated with a colorful pattern of swirls, vines, flowers, and leaves that appeared to have been designed by a cross-eyed maniac experiencing a bad acid trip.

Alice James and Jim Snow walked past rows of blackjack tables on the left and slot machines on the right, to the main bar on the east side of the casino.

One of the bartenders stood facing them, with his hands flat on the bar. Dressed in a white shirt, open at the collar, with a black vest, he was in his mid-thirties, with black hair and a mustache.

"We're looking for Tex," Snow said as they approached the bar.

"You've found him," the bartender said. He turned his head toward another man, who was stocking the beer cooler. "Ben. I'm taking five. Got it covered?"

"Covered." Without looking up, the other bartender continued loading beer bottles.

"You folks want anything to drink?"

"No, I'm good." Snow turned his head to Alice. She shook her head.

Tex led them to an empty table at the far end of the bar, out of the glare of the casino lights. The three of them pulled their chairs out and sat down.

"You're from Texas, I take it," Snow said.

"Nope," Tex said. "Just the name: Dallas Houston. My middle name is where I'm from. Dallas Denver Houston. When I was in high school, they called me 'Bus,' because when you say my full name, it sounds like an announcement in a bus terminal."

Alice smiled. "That's quite extraordinary."

Tex nodded. "My folks thought so. They were a couple of druggies, in the middle of a binge, I think, when they came up with it. They used to trot me out of my bedroom when they had company over and instruct me to tell them what my name was.

"I'd stand there like a talent show contestant and recite my full name, and they'd all toke up and laugh and congratulate my parents for being geniuses." He laughed.

"It is pretty clever, I think," Alice said. "At least they cared enough to take the time to think about it, instead of just picking something out of a short list."

"Yeah, I'll give them that," Tex said. "They weren't bad parents, I guess. They were never arrested after I was born, and my mother told me she cut way back on her drug intake while she was carrying me.

"My younger brother got a simpler name, and he got the shortened version of both of his names. On his birth certificate it says, 'Joe Sam Houston.' But he's happy with it."

"Denver's a nice city," Snow said. "I had considered moving there while I was still living up in Minnesota, but chose Las Vegas instead."

Tex smiled. "That's funny, because while I was living in Denver, I had considered moving to Minnesota. We spent our vacations up there, fishing—my ex-wife and I—back when we were still married. I finally decided I couldn't handle the winters."

Snow nodded. "The summers aren't all that spectacular either—unless you're a mosquito."

Tex laughed.

"You do any fishing down here?" Snow asked.

He shook his head. "I don't have a boat. I started saving for one when I got here, seven years ago. I got the kitty up to seventeen hundred dollars in the first three months. Now it's at thirteen hundred. I've got seven years' worth of boat research under my belt, but can't raise the down payment." He put his elbows on the table and interlaced his fingers. "I keep hoping I'll meet a woman someday who has a boat—but not much chance of that working in a place like this. I've never met a cocktail waitress yet who's even slightly interested in a boat."

"You've met a lot of them, I gather," Snow said.

"Cocktail waitresses? Sure. Who else but a bartender can fill their empty drink trays?" He laughed.

Snow smiled and nodded. "Speaking of cocktail waitresses, you say you worked quite a bit with Laura Roberts."

Tex's smile faded. "Yes. She filled her drink orders at this bar, and we worked the same shift most of the time."

"In the last year, do you ever remember her coming to work with a bruise on her face?"

"Yes, she did. She had a fairly big one on the left side of her jaw."

"Her left side?"

"Yep. Right here." He pointed to the left side of his jawbone, below his cheek.

"Do you remember when that was?"

"I don't remember exactly which day. But I remember it was a few days after Easter."

"So, that was a little over five months ago," Alice said.

Snow looked at her and nodded. "And if it was the left side of her face, Kevin Miller probably didn't hit her with the back of his hand. He's right handed. He could have hit with his left, but it's more likely someone who's right handed, who isn't a boxer, would use their right hand."

"Kevin Miller?" Tex said. "He was Laura's boyfriend, right?"

Snow nodded. "Yes, he was—off and on. Do you know him?"

"Not really," Tex said. "He came in here quite a few times looking for Laura. But she never wanted to talk to him. I could tell they'd broken up."

"Did Laura tell you how she got the bruise?" Alice said.

Tex shook his head. "Something like that—I'm not going to ask questions. I figure, if they want to tell me about it, they will. But she didn't say a word about it, and I didn't want to pry."

"Do you think Crystal Olson might have hit her?" Snow asked.

Tex jerked his head back, his eyes widening. "Crystal? Whoa—I don't think so. She's a pretty sweet girl. I can't imagine her hitting anyone."

"You know her pretty well?" Alice said.

"Dated her a few times. That was some time ago. A little over a year ago. She was always giving me the eye, so I finally asked her out. Nice lady."

"It didn't work out?" Alice asked.

Tex looked down at the table and laughed. "Oh it worked out great—until I did something incredibly stupid." He laughed again and shook his head.

"What happened?"

Tex looked up from the table at Alice. "It's a little embarrassing…"

Alice waited. Snow said nothing.

"It was our third date," Tex began. "Crystal invited me over for dinner. Laura didn't have any plans, so she was there. They were both off that night. We were sitting there listening to music and drinking wine, while Crystal's casserole was baking in the oven.

"We ran out of wine, and I volunteered to go pick up some more. But Crystal insisted she go. After some discussion about it, she finally left. And as soon as she got out the door, Laura kind of eased her way discreetly over to me, started putting her hands all over me, and complimented me on my choice of aftershave." He laughed. "It was Aqua Velva. I buy it when I do my grocery shopping.

"Anyway, I'm not sure what I was thinking, or if I even was, but the next thing I knew I was in Laura's bed with my clothes off. And then I heard Crystal's voice from the doorway to the bedroom. She said, 'At least you could have had the decency to shut the door.'"

"What did Crystal do then?" Snow asked.

"She just quietly turned around and walked back into the living room. I jumped out of bed and got my clothes back on and got out of there. When I walked past Crystal, she was sitting in a chair staring at the television. It wasn't even on."

"What happened after that?"

Tex sighed and folded his arms. "Of course, you know, there was no sense calling Crystal up again. That would be stupid. I was pretty sure she wouldn't want to go out with me again."

"Logical thinking," Alice said.

"But the next day at the start of our shift, Laura came up to me for her first load of drinks and asked me out. Just like that. She walked up to the bar and said, 'So, you want to go out with me?' I said, 'Sure.' I'm not proud of what happened, and I don't go around bragging about it, but I figured, what the hell?"

"How long did that last?" Alice said.

"Couple of weeks," Tex said. "I finally figured out she was living with some guy. I guess it was Kevin Miller. She wouldn't ever let me pick her up at her house. We'd always have to meet somewhere, or she'd come over to my place. And then one night, we were lying in bed, and her cell phone rang. She started arguing with him on the phone. Lied to him and told him she was out with Crystal. She told him he was an asshole for not trusting her." He laughed.

"Did you find out what happened between Laura and Crystal after you left that night?"

Tex nodded. "Laura told me she got dressed and went out to the living room. Crystal was still sitting there, staring at the TV. So Laura turned it on and sat down on the couch. They just sat there watching TV for the rest of the night. Laura said neither one of them said a word to each other."

Snow stared at Tex, frowning. "What happened to the casserole?" Snow said.

CHAPTER 21

All four chairs that occupied the James & James suite were still in Alice's office. Alice and Snow were seated in their swivel chairs, Alice behind her desk, Snow near the end of it. Crystal Olson and her mother were seated across the desk from Alice. They sat demurely, side by side, their hands clasped tightly in their laps, their eyes glassy and swollen. Looking at them caused Snow's shoulders to tense.

"I'm sure this won't be remembered by you as one of your favorite trips to Las Vegas, Ms. Olson," Alice said. "But we're hoping this investigation will be concluded soon. Then everyone involved can begin to put this experience behind them."

With a forced smile, Kathy Olson nodded. "Please—you can call me Kathy, Alice. And I would just like to say, at this point, that I'm pleased two competent detectives such as yourselves are working on this case to get it resolved. I don't have anything bad to say about the police in general, but I'm pretty sure most of them don't take much of an interest in seeing justice done. I know in the case of my late husband, rest his soul, there was a less than stellar job done investigating his death. And I'd hate to see the same thing happen a second time with Laura."

Snow shifted his gaze to Crystal. She was biting her upper lip and staring at the front surface of Alice's desk.

"Thank you, Kathy," Alice said. "We appreciate your confidence in us. And I'm sure Crystal must appreciate your support during a difficult time like this. It can't be easy for you having to take off from your teaching duties. I'm guessing that school has started for your students in Omaha?"

She nodded. "It started a couple of weeks ago. The principal I work for is very understanding, and we always manage to bring in some talented substitutes, so it's not that much of a problem." She nodded again.

"Oh, that's good to hear," Alice said. "One thing I'd like to make you aware of: we don't expect to have any questions for you. Of course, there is a chance we may think of some in the future. But at the present time, I'd like to let you know that it's not important that you be here for these interviews with Crystal—unless you want to, and that's fine, of course."

Kathy Olson nodded. "Thanks, Alice. Truthfully, I don't know what to do with myself. And I'd like to help in some way, even if it's nothing more than providing moral support for Crystal."

Alice smiled. "Okay. That's perfectly fine." She shifted her eyes to Crystal and sat back in her chair. "Crystal, first of all, I'd like to congratulate you on your upcoming wedding."

Crystal brought her eyes up. "Oh…thank you…well, it's not definite yet."

"Really. I'm sorry to hear that," Alice said. She glanced at Crystal's left hand. "I noticed you haven't been wearing an engagement ring, so I was surprised to hear you and Andrew Tully had set a date."

"We didn't set a date, really," Crystal said. "Just a month and year—more like an approximation."

"I see. So Kevin hasn't given you a ring yet?"

Crystal's shoulders sagged a little. "Yes, he did give me a ring. But we've been going back and forth about it."

"Since you're not wearing the ring," Alice said, "it looks to me like you've called off the wedding."

Kathy Olson's eyes narrowed. "What is this about—exactly?"

"Kathy, I apologize if it seems like I'm asking impertinent questions, and maybe I am. But this how we have to do this. We ask a lot of what may seem like stupid questions. We do that all day long, every day, until we hit on something. And then we change direction."

Kathy Olson continued to stare at Alice, frowning. She said nothing more.

Alice turned her eyes back to Crystal and waited.

Crystal sighed. "I didn't call off the wedding officially. We've just been having issues lately, and I haven't felt like wearing the engagement ring. I still have it. I didn't give it back to him."

Snow thought about his two ex-wives. He wondered what had happened to the wedding rings he'd bought for them. Probably converted into a couple of expensive ankle bracelets. Or put on display in trophy cases.

He brought his mind back into focus. "Crystal," he said, "Alice and I were going over Laura's recent cell phone records, and we noticed a lot of calls to and from your fiancé. Do you have any idea what that was about?"

Crystal's expression remained unaffected. She thought for a moment and then shook her head. "I honestly have no idea."

"More than thirty phone calls in the two weeks leading up to the murder," Snow said. "Doesn't that surprise you?"

She shrugged. "I don't know. Are you suggesting they were having an affair?"

130

"What do you think about the possibility of that?" Snow said.

"If they were, I didn't know anything about it. Maybe they were planning something."

"Do you have a birthday coming up?"

She frowned. "No."

Her eyes grew moist. She reached up and scratched her forehead with her thumbnail. Lowering her hand back into her lap, she began to cry. "Actually, it's quite possible. Kevin Miller, originally, was my boyfriend. I met him through an online dating site. After a few weeks, he lost interest in me and started going out with Laura. It happened that way with nearly every guy I dated. Laura kept stealing them all away from me. Can't say as I blame them. Look at me—I'm short and dumpy. Laura was tall and beautiful."

"Don't sell yourself short," Snow said. "I think you're quite attractive."

She looked down at her hands and shrugged.

"Crystal, were you aware of any abusive behavior between Kevin and Laura?" Alice asked.

Crystal leveled her gaze on Alice. "Like what?"

"Did Kevin ever hit her?"

"Not that I know of."

"Do you remember seeing a bruise on her face?"

She thought for a moment. "No."

"Did you ever hit her?"

Kathy Olson jumped up out of her seat. "Now, just one minute! I'd like to know what's going on here!" She put her hands on her hips, her eyes burning fire at Alice.

"We're just asking a lot of different questions," Alice said, evenly. "I know it seems harsh and intrusive, but we always work this way."

"It looks to me like you're trying to build a case against my daughter! She didn't do anything wrong. If you ask me, you should be interrogating Andrew Tully. Not Crystal."

"We have been interviewing Andrew," Alice said. "And we plan to interview him further—along with everyone else we can think of. We have to ask a lot of pointed questions, Kathy. It doesn't mean we consider Crystal a suspect. The truth is we really don't have any suspects yet. And we won't get anywhere if we just sit and discuss the weather."

"No suspects? Not yet you don't," Kathy Olson said. "But it looks to me like you're putting the foundation in place to build this whole case around my daughter. And I won't *stand* for it!"

"Good," Snow chimed in. He motioned toward her chair. "Would you please *sit* for it?"

She turned her glare to Snow. "Was that supposed to be funny, you incompetent jerk?"

"Kathy," Alice insisted, "if you don't sit down and remain quiet, we'll have to ask you to leave."

"I'll leave alright," Kathy snapped. "And I'll take my daughter with me."

"If she wants to go," Alice said, "we can't force her to stay. But the truth will come out sooner or later, with her help or without it."

"What truth?" Kathy waved her hand toward Alice. "This trumped-up stack of fabrication you're attempting to hammer together? You're both incompetent. A couple of two-bit morons who can't hold a regular job—so you have to resort to this type of work. You're both a couple of lowlifes. You should be ashamed of yourselves!"

Alice sighed and turned her head to Crystal. "Would you mind answering my question, Crystal?"

She was staring at the floor, her eyes glazed, the color gone from her cheeks. "I never hit Laura."

She reached up and scratched her forehead with her thumbnail.

"That's it," Kathy said. "You have your answer. You've asked enough questions. We're leaving." She reached down and gripped her daughter's arm, pulling her up out of her chair.

Kathy turned and shoved Crystal toward the door.

In the hallway, she threw a final look toward Alice. "Idiots!" she said.

The front door slammed hard enough to shake the building, and they were gone.

Snow looked at Alice. "That was quite enjoyable. Could you remind me what it is about this job that we like?"

"I'll try to think of something," she said.

CHAPTER 22

"Tully Dental." It was a female voice, youthful and cheery.

"Good morning," Snow said. "I was wondering if Dr. Tully is taking on new patients."

"Yes, he is," she said. "Would you like to set up an appointment?"

"Well," Snow said, "I'm not sure. You see, Dr. Tully was recommended to me by a friend. I had been having problems with my previous dentist. And I had been with her for a long time—over ten years."

"That's quite a while," she said. "What happened?"

"Well," Snow said, "in the beginning she was very good. She was careful, and gentle, and painless. I was very happy with her for quite a few years. But over time, she seemed to change. As she got older, she became careless and rough. One time I had a deep cavity, and she didn't numb it sufficiently. I didn't realize until she got down around the bottom of the tooth with the drill that she hadn't injected enough Novocain."

"Oh no."

"Yeah, she must have noticed my discomfort, because she stopped drilling and asked me if it was numb enough. I didn't want her stabbing me with that giant needle again and waiting around for another half hour while she wandered into another room and started torturing somebody else. So I told her it was fine and just endured the pain."

"That's terrible," she said.

"Yes, it was," Snow said. "But I soon put it to the back of my mind. However, the next time I went in for an exam, she was rougher than ever. She looked terrible, with bags under her eyes, and she told me I was lucky she was in a good mood.

"After the examination, she told me my teeth were okay, but six of my fillings were old and would need to be replaced. She said two of the fillings were so large they would require crowns."

"Uh-oh."

"I asked her if the fillings were still functional—if we could possibly put it off for a while longer. Because fillings are like tires, I've been told. They don't last forever, so I didn't want to replace them until I had gotten full use out of them. Otherwise, they would have to be replaced again at an earlier date than necessary."

"That's true," she said.

"Well," Snow said, "she told me the fillings were still sealed, and they hadn't broken down at all. But still, they were old, and it was her recommendation that they be replaced immediately.

"It was then that it dawned on me that she must have developed a gambling problem recently and needed the money."

"Oh…"

"So I told her I'd keep that in mind for the next visit. But that was over a year ago, and I haven't been back. Now I'm pretty sure it's best to let another dentist have a whack at me."

"You haven't been to a dentist in over a year?" she said. "That's not good. It's best to come in every six months for an examination and cleaning."

"That's what I've been told," Snow said.

"Then would you like to go ahead and set up an appointment?"

"Let me explain the problem to you," Snow said.

"Okay."

"I told this friend of mine that I was looking for a new dentist, and he recommended Dr. Tully."

"He is very good," she said. "Dr. Tully works on my teeth, and he's very gentle and only does the work that's necessary. He doesn't do any gouging."

"That's exactly what my friend told me," Snow said. "So I had decided to go ahead and begin to prepare myself mentally for an office visit. I'm kind of a coward when it comes to trips to the dentist—so that can take several weeks."

"Well, I was almost to the point of picking up the phone and making an appointment, and then my friend called me out of the blue and told me to forget it. He told me to find another dentist."

"Oh, you're kidding! What happened?"

"He told me he'd made an appointment well in advance and went to a lot of trouble making arrangements with his boss for the time off. And that's always a hassle for him because his boss is overbearing and doesn't like anyone taking time off from work for personal reasons. My friend explained that dentists are usually only open during working hours. He goes through that every time with the guy."

"That's terrible," she agreed.

"Anyway, he was getting ready to leave work to go to his appointment when somebody called him from your office and told him his visit would have to be postponed for another day."

"Oh, that's right," she said. "Yes, that was me who called. That was last Tuesday, right?"

"I believe it was."

"Yes," she said. "Dr. Tully had an emergency and had to leave around noon that day. I had to call everyone and try to reschedule. I was sure everyone rescheduled while I had them on the phone, if I remember correctly. It seemed to me like everyone was pleased about it. I don't remember anyone being ticked off. What is your friend's name?"

"Actually, I think it would be best not to give it," Snow said. "It's a sticky situation. I think he might be upset to know that I called and talked to you about all of this. I wouldn't want you to call him and try to win him back and have him find out that I called. Then he'd be angry with me."

"Oh, I wouldn't do that," she said. "I'm just wondering now because I thought I rescheduled all of those appointments over the phone that day..."

"Anyway," Snow said. "I was wondering what sort of emergency it was that caused all this rescheduling. As a prospective new patient, I wouldn't want to rush into anything if I have doubts. You know, I would hate to go to the trouble of filling out all the forms and everything, only to up and change dentists again because of future cancellations."

"Oh, it doesn't happen often," she insisted. "Hardly ever."

"Really?"

"Only twice in the last year, and both of those times were within the last three weeks. Before that—I don't remember the last time there was a rescheduling."

"Did the doctor have a problem at home or something?" Snow asked.

"No, nothing like that," she said. "He's not married. In fact, he's engaged, and I shouldn't say this, but it probably had something to do with that."

"In what way?" Snow asked.

"When he left," she said, "he seemed really happy and invigorated. Full of nervous energy. You know what I mean? I think he was off to meet his fiancée."

"I see," Snow said.

"I shouldn't have said anything," she said. "But I think when two people are in love like that, and they're just starting out their new life together, it's good to make allowances for them. I hope that if it ever happens to me, people would feel that way. Don't you think?"

"Yes," Snow agreed. "I think that's a good idea. Love is, after all, a many-splendored thing."

She giggled. "Yes, it is. Okay," she said, "so when would you like to come in for your first visit?"

"Hmm," Snow said. "That's a good question. I'm looking at my schedule, and I don't see an opening anywhere for the next couple weeks. I think there may be a possibility the following week on that Thursday…"

"Is that October seventh?"

"Yes. Yes, it is."

"What time would be convenient for you?"

"The problem is," Snow said, "now that I look at it, I'm pretty sure I scheduled a meeting for that day and neglected to enter it in my planner. I'll have to call the gentleman and find out which day the meeting is scheduled for and get back to you."

"Okay, you can call me back. That's fine."

"The problem is," Snow said, "he's in Bangladesh, and it's getting late there. I have a policy never to call anyone after nine p.m.—but I'll shoot him an e-mail and find out as soon as he replies."

"Okay," she said. "Call back when you find out."

"I'll do that," Snow said. "Hopefully I'll figure out where I put his e-mail address and phone number."

"And may I have you name?" She said.

"Definitely," Snow said. "It's Hubert Hatchway. It's spelled just like it sounds."

CHAPTER 23

"We need more chairs."

Snow surveyed the office. He was sitting in his swivel chair at the end of Alice's desk. His elbows were positioned on the arm rests, his fingers interlocked in front of his chest. "It looks to me like this office is full of chairs."

"Every chair in the suite is in here," Alice said. "What's in your office? Just an empty desk and a phone. We should have two client chairs in each office and four chairs in the reception area."

"We aren't even using the reception area," Snow argued. "We don't have a receptionist. Why would anyone be sitting in the reception area? It's not likely there will ever be a line of people waiting to get in here to see us. And I don't even use my office. I've only been in there three times: the first time to look at it; the second time to plug in the phone and put my two chairs in there; the third time to get the chairs and put them in here. In fact, I'm not even sure what use I could make of my office. I'm always in here with you."

"We need to give the impression that there's a lot going on here," Alice said. "People walk in and see an empty reception area, and they'll think we don't get many cases."

"They'd be right," Snow said. He lifted his commuter mug from her desk and took a sip of coffee. "But I see your point. When we get a chance, we could go to Costco and pick up more chairs, a small end table to put magazines on. And maybe we should get a mannequin."

"For what?"

"We could put it behind the counter and dress it really nice—give the impression we have a receptionist."

Alice laughed. "We should get three. Two of them could be sitting in the chairs, reading magazines."

Snow nodded and took another sip of coffee. "Now you're talking."

"What did you find out about Andrew Tully?" Alice said.

Snow set his mug on the desk and settled back in his chair. "I called his office. Found out he cancelled all of his appointments for the afternoon and left around noon on Tuesday. His receptionist said he was zipping around, full of glee before he left. She assumed he was heading off to a romantic encounter with his fiancée. But Crystal never mentioned seeing him that day."

Alice opened her top desk drawer, took out a thin stack of papers, and set them in front of her. She studied the top sheet for a moment and then looked at Snow. "Laura made a call to Tully's cell phone at eleven forty that morning."

Snow looked at his watch. "I wonder if Dr. Tully has an open slot this morning. I think we should schedule an office visit."

The cell phone in Snow's pocket chirped.

He pulled it out, flipped it open, and issued his standard greeting: "Yeah."

"Mr. Snow?"

"Yes."

"This is Kathy Olson."

"Oh, hello, Kathy. I didn't recognize your number. What can I do for you today?"

Her voice sounded shaky and strained. "I'm calling to apologize, Mr. Snow, for the way I acted last night. I was very upset at the time, what with everything that has happened. Crystal has been under a lot of stress from this, and it has taken its toll on me too. We've just been sitting around this motel room and the pool, waiting to find out who did this terrible thing. And it's impossible to relax. I hope you understand."

"Of course we do, Kathy. If I were in your situation, I imagine I would react the same way. It's only natural. We are human, after all, and it's good to let out a burst of emotion now and then to release the inner tension. I think it's not a bad idea to go outside and let go with a good primal scream now and then, just to keep the blood pressure in check."

Kathy seemed to relax, her voice evening out. She sighed, as if relieved. "Thank you for being so understanding, Mr. Snow."

"Call me Jim," Snow said. "When anyone calls me Mr. Snow, I feel like a character in a children's book."

She forced a laugh. "That's funny. You're very clever. And I want you to know—Crystal and I both do—if you ever need any help from us, give us a call. If we can't answer your questions over the phone, we'd be pleased to stop by your office."

"That's fantastic, Kathy. We'll keep that in mind. And I want to assure you and Crystal that you have no reason to worry."

"Worry about what, Jim?"

"Well," Snow said, "I mean to say that I don't believe the perpetrator will be targeting Crystal at all. I don't think she's in any danger of any sort. I think this crime only had to do with Laura."

"Oh!" Kathy said. "Well, that's reassuring. I'll tell Crystal. She'll be relieved to hear that. And pass my apology on to Alice, please."

"Will do," Snow said. "Thanks for calling, Kathy."

Snow snapped the phone shut and shoved it in his front pocket.

"That was Kathy Olson?" Alice said.

Snow swiveled his chair facing her. "She called to apologize," he said.

"That was nice of her," Alice said.

"She thinks I'm clever," Snow said, smiling.

"I wondered why you were so charming on the phone."

"You just haven't noticed," Snow said. "The grumpy exterior is just a cover for the real me. It's impossible to keep it buried all the time. In this business it pays to act a little bit tough. It's hard to get new business if a man goes around acting like Liberace all the time."

Tully Dental was situated in a small office complex in east Las Vegas. As Alice and Snow approached the door to the office, Andrew Tully came rushing out through the doorway, shutting the door quickly behind him.

"Good morning," he said, feigning a buoyant tone. "It's a nice morning; I thought we could walk over to the park and talk. It's right across the street."

"Alright," Alice said.

They turned and walked with him, Alice and Tully side by side on the sidewalk, Snow treading alongside on the grass.

"Can you believe this weather?" Tully said with a slight flutter in his voice. He reminded Snow of a teenager on his first date.

"Yes," Snow said. "It seems to have been cooler than normal the last few days."

"Probably won't last much longer," Tully added. "Indian summer usually hits about now, and it climbs back up above a hundred for a while."

Alice turned her head to Tully. "I hope we're not taking you away from your patients, Andrew."

"Oh no," he said. "I'm free until after lunch. Monday mornings always seem a little slow for me. I wonder if my patients fear that I won't be at my best after a couple days off, or if they're not in the mood to deal with dental work so early in the week."

"I don't think I've ever been in the mood to deal with dental work," Snow said.

Tully forced a weak laugh.

"Speaking of time off," Alice said, "Jim and I were wondering what caused you to suddenly cancel all of your appointments last Tuesday afternoon?"

"Oh." Tully lowered his gaze to the sidewalk in front of him. "Last Tuesday. That was…" He paused. "I wasn't feeling well."

"Your receptionist told me you had personal business to take care of," Snow said.

"Yes, personal business," Tully said. "Going home sick *is* personal business."

"She said you were practically doing the soft-shoe out the door when you left. It didn't sound to me like you were sick."

"She said that? Well, I always try to maintain an upbeat attitude while I'm at the office. I think it's good for business and morale."

"Andrew," Alice said, "are you hiding something?"

"*Hiding* something? No, of course not. What would I be hiding?"

"We noticed that Laura made a call to your cell phone twenty minutes before you decided to cancel the rest of your appointments," Alice said. "Was there something she said that made you ill?"

"Something she said? No—of course not." He let out a short laugh that sounded more like he was choking.

"Why did Laura call you, Andrew?"

"Why? I don't remember specifically. Actually, I think she just called to talk. You know how women are. They don't always need a reason to call someone. Every woman I've ever dated has been that way." His face began to redden. "I heard about a study that determined the average phone call a man makes amounts to only a few minutes, whereas for women it's much longer. Half an hour or longer—I forgot..."

"You're terrible at lying, Andrew," Alice observed. "Sooner or later, we'll find out about it. Why don't you just tell us the truth? We'll respect your privacy, unless we find it has something to do with Laura's murder."

Tully clenched his teeth, looked straight ahead for a moment, and shook his head forcefully like a horse with ear mites. "Shit," he said. Lowering his gaze back to the sidewalk, he sighed. "Alright, you're bound to find out anyway. I don't know what came over me, but I will confess I've experienced a few episodes of indiscretion recently. I don't know what brought it on—possibly premarital jitters. But I have to admit to being weak. And Laura Roberts was very seductive. I couldn't control myself around her."

The threesome stopped at the corner, waiting for the light to change.

"How long had this been going on?" Alice said.

His shoulders slouching, Tully stared across the street at a picnic table in the park. "Not long. A few weeks. Laura was always friendly toward me in her own way—kindness and caring intermingled with occasional insults and bouts of meanness. But gradually, she started becoming more and more forward, until it reached the point…" He sighed. "It started the day she asked me to give her a ride to the dealership to pick up her car. We were on the way there, stopped at an intersection, waiting for the light to change. She was sitting extremely close. We ended up kissing, somehow. And at every stoplight after that. We eventually found ourselves at my place. Didn't even pick up her car that day."

"So, last Tuesday," Snow said, "you left at noon. And you went directly over to Laura's place?"

"Laura's place?" Tully said. "No. She…uh…she came to my house."

The light changed, and they began to cross the street.

"What time did she leave your home?"

"What time?" He shrugged and raised his hands in front of him. "Oh, I guess it was around two thirty."

"She left by herself?"

He lowered his hands and nodded. "Yes…yes, by herself."

"And where was she going? Did she say?"

He shook his head. "Where? Home. She said she was going home. Of course, I can't be sure that she actually went directly home."

"Might have stopped to pick up some milk?" Snow said.

Tully squeaked out a laugh.

In the park, they walked across the grass to the nearest picnic table and sat down, Alice and Snow on one side, Tully across the table from them. He was trying to smile, but he looked as though he might cry.

"After Laura left your house," Snow said, "what did you do, Dr. Tully?"

"Well," he said, "as soon as she drove off, I got in my car and went down to the Strip. My favorite hangout is the Royal Palace Casino. Have you ever been there?"

Snow nodded. "What time did you get there?"

"It was about three o'clock."

"Did you talk to anyone? Can anybody verify it?"

"Oh yes," Tully said. "I'm a regular there. I use my player's card, always. And the bartenders know me. I always sit at the main bar and play video poker. You get drinks faster that way."

"It's not that we think you had anything to do with Laura's death," Alice insisted. "We just need to check on everyone who knew Laura and came in contact with her."

Tully nodded. "I understand. You can ask the bartenders—they should remember me."

"Dr. Tully," Snow said, "do you think there is any chance Crystal might have found out about your fling with Laura?"

"Crystal?" Tully said. "I don't think so."

"How did she act toward you after the murder?" Snow said.

Tully shrugged. "I actually haven't talked to her since last Monday night."

Snow glanced at Alice and returned his gaze to Tully. "Why is that?"

He shrugged again. "I don't know. She hasn't called me, and I thought she might need some time to deal with this."

"You didn't feel like calling to console her?" Alice said.

Tully scratched the side of his head. "It's just that—we've been having problems…"

"Dr. Tully," Snow said, "how do you think Crystal would react if she found out you were having an affair with Laura?"

"Oh." Tully raised his eyebrows. "No doubt she'd be upset."

"Did Crystal and Laura ever get into it, physically?"

"What do you mean?"

"A physical altercation. They ever come to blows?"

"You mean—like punch each other?"

Snow nodded.

Tully shrugged. "Not that I know of."

"You ever see Laura with a bruise on her jaw?"

Tully's eyes narrowed. "Bruise on her jaw? I never noticed one. No."

Back in the car, Snow turned his head to Alice. "How are we supposed to figure this out with everyone lying about everything? This is about the worst I've ever seen it—and that guy takes the cake. How would you like to have him for your dentist?"

"If everyone told the truth," Alice said, "there would be no need for investigators. The perpetrator would always confess."

Snow slipped the key into the ignition and cranked the engine to life. "Most of the cases I handled in homicide—that was exactly what happened. The suspect would either confess at the murder scene, his home, or in the interview room. I still managed to stay pretty busy."

Alice nodded. "I'm pretty sure he was lying about Laura coming over to his house Tuesday afternoon. That woman seemed to enjoy the risk of getting caught. I think it gave her a thrill. I suspect Andrew met her at her house. Crystal came home early from work with a headache—remember?"

"You think Crystal might have caught them in bed together?"

"It's possible," Alice said. "It's one of the leading motivators—for murder."

"You're right. Food for thought," Snow said, shifting into reverse. "You know what I'm thinking?"

"Jim," she said, "I'm not in the mood for another buffet."

CHAPTER 24

The main bar at the Royal Palace Casino was shaped like a rectangular racetrack. It was situated in the middle of the gambling floor for easy access.

After leaving Alice to the task of talking with casino security about Tully's player card activity, Snow walked up to the nearest of the two bartenders. He appeared to be in his mid-twenties, clean-cut, with short brown hair and an easy smile. He wore the uniform burgundy shirt with a gold nametag that read *Ricky*.

Snow introduced himself and explained about the investigation. The bartender provided a firm handshake and the name Ricky Dows.

Snow stood with his hands in his back pockets. "You know a fellow by the name of Andrew Tully, Ricky?"

"I sure do," Ricky said. "He comes in here a couple times a week or more." He turned and pointed to the end of the bar. "He always sits at one of those three slot machines. Always plays video poker, and usually drinks gin martinis, up, with no olives."

"Was he in here last Tuesday afternoon?"

Dows looked over his left shoulder at the bar and thought for a moment. "Let's see. It was either Tuesday or Wednesday.

I'm off Sundays and Mondays, and it seems to me like it was the first day of my work week. So that would be Tuesday—but I can't swear to it."

"He was using his player's card in the slot machine—did you notice?"

Dows turned his head back facing Snow. "Oh yeah, he always shoves that thing in there as soon as he sits down. Everybody does. I guess they want the points. But most of the guests seem to believe they won't get free drinks unless they use their card, which isn't the case. The only rule they have here is that you can't call the brand without the card. So that's a good reason to use a player's card—along with the points."

Snow nodded. "Plus you save two bucks per person on the buffet."

Dows grinned. "What a deal, huh?"

"So, you say Andrew Tully was here Tuesday or Wednesday of last week?"

"Now that I think about it," Dows said, "I'm pretty sure it was Tuesday."

"Do you know what time it was when he got here?"

"Middle of the afternoon, I think it was. I start at noon. And I seem to remember him coming in earlier than usual. Seemed like only a few hours after I started. Usually he gets here around five thirty or six. I'm off at eight, and he's usually still here when I leave."

"What about Tuesday night?" Snow asked.

"Yeah, he was still here, pounding them down like there'd be no tomorrow."

"He was drinking pretty heavy that day?"

"Oh yeah. We had trouble keeping his glass filled."

"Does he usually drink that heavily?"

Dows shrugged and tilted his head. "Sometimes, if there's something bugging him. Otherwise he drinks at an average pace—maybe a couple drinks per hour."

Snow frowned and folded his arms in front of him. "Was there something bothering him last Tuesday night?"

Dows nodded. "He was really nervous when he got here. Seemed jittery. Sweating a lot. Fidgeting. Couldn't seem to get comfortable. Seemed really irritable."

"He's not usually like that?" Snow asked.

Dows shook his head. "No. He's a nervous kind of guy. High strung, I guess. But I don't remember ever seeing him like that."

"How long have you known him?"

"A year," Dows said. "That's the length of time I've worked here."

Snow nodded. "Where'd you work before that?"

"Tacoma, Washington," Dows said.

"Really? Tending bar up there?"

Dows let out a breath and shook his head. "I had a moving business up there."

"What happened with that?" Snow unfolded his arms and sat down in one of the padded bar chairs.

Dows put his hands on the inside lip of the bar and leaned against it. "Belly up," he said, looking down at his knuckles. "I'm originally from Oregon. Grew up there. My family was into surveying. But that went down the tubes when the housing market went bust. So I took all the savings I had and started a moving business up in Tacoma. Bought my own moving truck and all the equipment to go with it."

"Why did you pick that neck of the woods?" Snow asked.

"I liked it there, and it's a fairly large city."

"You had some friends from Oregon go up there with you?"

Dows shook his head. "No, I went up there alone; hired a guy to work with me. We couldn't get enough business to make a go of it, so I had to lay him off and try to figure out what to do next." He pushed back from the bar and put his hands in his front pockets. "I had the impression Las Vegas was the place to go when you need a fresh start. So I borrowed some money from my folks, moved down here, and went to bartender school."

"And they hired you here a year ago with no experience?" Snow said.

"I had the bartender training," Dows said.

"But everyone's been cutting back and laying off. Unemployment here has been over fourteen percent for a long time."

Dows raised his eyebrows and shrugged.

"What'd you do with your moving truck?" Snow asked.

"I've got it in storage in Oregon at my uncle's place."

"I think you should get it and bring it down here," Snow said. "People are moving out of Las Vegas in droves. They're showing up at U-Haul without reservations, looking for anything they can rent—to get the hell out of here. It seems to me the moving business should be booming here right now, as long as you don't mind driving cross-country."

Dows smiled. "You could be right. But now that I've got some income, I think I'd better stay put with this job for now. I'll watch and see how it plays out."

Snow felt a hand on his shoulder and turned to see Alice standing next to him.

"What did you find out?" he asked her.

"He started playing at 3:07 p.m.—and didn't leave until 8:56, Tuesday evening."

"I guess we can cross him off the list of possibles," Snow said. He looked at Dows and pointed a thumb at Alice. "My associate, Alice James."

Dows shook her hand, and she sat down next to Snow.

On the other side of the bar, an old man with a white beard, a cowboy hat, and hunched shoulders raised his glass and rattled the ice in it. "Barkeep!" he said.

"Looks like you need to get back to work," Snow said.

"You need anything more from me?" Dows asked.

Snow shook his head. "If I think of something, I know where to find you. Good luck with your moving business."

Dows smiled and headed off toward the old man.

Snow turned his head to Alice. "Did you want to order anything while we're here?"

"I'm fine," she said.

"The bartender told me Tully was agitated and drinking more than usual Tuesday afternoon—and evening."

"That's interesting," Alice said. "What do you think caused that? You would think he'd have been relaxed after his encounter with the seductress."

Snow turned his head back to the front and watched Dows mixing the old man's drink. "Well, looking at the facts, he got a call from Laura. Left work happy and excited, on his way to meet her. Then he showed up here three hours later, nervous, on edge, and definitely not happy. What does that tell us?"

"You think Laura broke it off with him?"

Snow turned his eyes back toward Alice. "That's one possibility. Another is that he got caught."

Alice nodded. "Then he came here to try and figure out what to do."

"Or just let off steam and drown his sorrows," Snow said.

"Or maybe give himself an alibi," Alice suggested.

Snow nodded. "I think, at this point, we should focus on Crystal Olson. I'd like to talk to some people who know her, who aren't necessarily close friends. It's hard to get the truth out of people who have an interest in protecting someone."

"She has a Facebook page," Alice said. "I didn't look at it very closely, but I did notice quite a few friends on it. I'd like to go back to the office and research some of them, see if we can find anyone local who's willing to tell us about her. Someone with an objective viewpoint."

"You're on Facebook?" Snow asked.

"Of course," Alice said. "It's very useful."

"I thought mostly teenagers used that site."

"Jim," Alice said, "even my mother is on Facebook. She must have a couple hundred friends."

"No kidding. Does she Twitter, too?"

"No, Jim. She tweets." Alice smiled.

Snow raised an eyebrow. "And I was happy that I'd recently gotten to the point where I understood e-mail."

CHAPTER 25

Dr. Nancy Gilmore maintained her office in a remodeled three-bedroom home off Spring Mountain Road a few miles west of I-15. A graduate of UCLA, she was a respected clinical psychologist with a Web site so complicated it locked up Alice's computer. She had tried three times to access it, with no luck. She found the only way out was to reboot.

Dr. Gilmore, an attractive woman in her early forties, with short blonde hair, met Alice and Snow at the front door. She wore a navy blue pantsuit and low heels. She escorted them to her office, a combination of two bedrooms with a wall removed. It was furnished with an oak desk, a stuffed couch, and two matching chairs. The walls and carpet were subtle earth tones, complementing the various potted plants surrounding the furniture. Soft lighting from the ceiling accentuated the wood-framed paintings of lakes, mountains, prairies, and cities. The ambience felt cozy, and Snow could feel it melding with his inner being.

Alice and Snow seated themselves on the couch, with Dr. Gilmore settling into one of the chairs to the side of it. The furniture arrangement forced them to turn their heads to the left to look at her.

Dr. Gilmore smiled. "So…you're private detectives…"

Alice and Snow smiled and nodded.

"That's interesting. I've never met anyone who worked in that field." She fixed her gaze on Alice. "And how did you manage to establish yourself in that profession, Alice?"

Alice sat perfectly straight, knees together, feet flat on the floor. She resembled a prospective employee at a job interview. "I started out in Metro as a patrol officer," she said. "When I was eligible, I took the test and was promoted into Homicide as a detective. That's where I got my experience."

Dr. Gilmore's smile broadened. "That's admirable. So you decided to spread your wings and broaden your career, gaining independence in the process. Congratulations, Alice."

Alice grinned happily. "Why thank you, Dr. Gilmore."

Dr. Gilmore swung her head toward Snow. "And how about you, Jim?"

Snow cleared his throat. "I was in Homicide," he said. "I quit the force to play poker for a living."

Dr. Gilmore's eyes narrowed. "I see." She waved her limp hand in a circle in front of her. "Was this some sort of compulsion you were dealing with?"

Snow could feel his face heating up. "No, of course not. I studied the game and played extensively for quite a while on the side while I was still with Metro. I kept detailed records of wins and losses. Then I established a business plan, complete with an estimation of the longest losing streak I might have to endure. My bankroll was more than adequate—so I tendered my resignation and went to work as a professional poker player."

Dr. Gilmore's eyes widened, and the corners of her mouth curled up. She looked like the Cheshire cat, waiting to pounce. "And how did it go for you?" she asked.

"For the first two and a half years I did pretty good," Snow said. "I had a few short periods of consolidation, but showed a profit overall during that time."

She rested her chin on the knuckle of her index finger and nodded slowly. "And after that?"

Snow fidgeted in his chair. "Then, for the next six months, I lost steadily. Nearly every day. I lost my confidence, decided to take a break from it—and investigate my brother-in-law's murder. After of few more months of loafing around, Alice broached the idea of this partnership we entered into. I had no other prospects, so I decided to give it a shot."

Leaning back in her chair, Dr. Gilmore folded her hands in her lap. "It sounds like you're saying that Alice threw you a lifeline, and you took it."

"I guess you could put it that way," Snow said.

"And how is the private detective business working out for you, Jim?"

Snow shrugged. "It's a mixed bag," he said. "To be honest, at this point I'm not too sure I'm crazy about it."

Dr. Gilmore nodded and then turned her head toward Alice. "I'm curious, Alice—how you feel about that."

Alice sighed. "Well. You know…I'd actually rather not say."

Dr. Gilmore tilted her head. "Why not?"

"I don't think it's a good idea," Alice said.

"Honesty and open conversation," Dr. Gilmore said, "is always a good idea. Why not clear the air?"

Alice shrugged. "Sometimes I feel like I want to smack him upside the head."

"What do you think about that, Jim?" Dr. Gilmore shot him a sidelong look.

Snow raised an eyebrow and turned it toward Alice. "No comment," he replied.

"You'll have to forgive me for being so personal." Dr. Gilmore spread her hands and chuckled. "I do get carried away and forget myself sometimes. I'm used to dealing with my patients all day, every day. But I have to say, I have never met a couple who present such a striking contrast."

She motioned her hand toward Alice. "Here we have an elegant, charming woman in a business suit…" She nodded toward Snow. "And next to her, a fellow with mussed hair, jeans, and—what is that—a golf shirt, with the tail untucked?"

"It's the style of the shirt," Snow said. "It has slits in the sides; I assume it's designed to be worn this way. Although I could be wrong; it didn't come with instructions. As for my hair, we were driving with the windows down. It always does that to my hair. Maybe I should wear a hat. A fedora possibly, or a top hat with a big bow tie. I might add that we live in an age dominated by casual attire. Anytime I see a man in a tie—other than at weddings and funerals—that's a flag, telling me he's trying to sell something. I'm not selling anything, Dr. Gilmore. And I like to be comfortable—without a colorful noose tied around my neck, strangling me.

"But enough about me. We seem to have gotten off on a tangent. Would you mind if we talk about someone you know? That is, after all, the purpose of our visit."

Dr. Gilmore offered a smirk, blinked slowly, and nodded. "Certainly. I apologize, Jim. Whom would you like to know about?"

"Crystal Olson," Snow said.

"Nice, energetic young lady," Dr. Gilmore said. "She works as a cocktail waitress at Shillington's Casino. One of the best shortstops I have ever seen in women's amateur softball. And given a decent pitch, she can knock the cover off the ball."

"Is she a friend of yours?" Alice asked.

"What is an accurate definition of 'friend' these days?" Dr. Gilmore said. "Everyone seems to be friends with as many people as possible. The more friends one has, the more successful they seem. And now they can be displayed on the Internet for the entire world to see and tallied up like a herd of cattle.

"Crystal Olson and I don't seem to have much in common, other than a love for the game of softball. So we don't attend the same social functions, and we don't pal around together. Her batting average is better than mine, but I try not to be envious of her for that.

"We've played on the same teams for years, her at shortstop, me at first base. We work together like gears in a fine watch. And we play year-round."

"Has she ever seemed overly aggressive to you?" Alice said.

"No."

"Temperamental?"

"No. She's always in control of herself. If anything, I would say she leans toward the personality of a wallflower. If there is any anger inside her, she uses it constructively when necessary—during the swing of her bat."

"Has she ever swung it at any of the other players?" Snow asked.

"Never."

"Do you think she could be provoked to the point of killing someone?"

"With Crystal—not possible."

Snow glanced at Alice. She shook her head.

"We'd like to thank you for your time, Dr. Gilmore," Snow said. "I know you must be busy. We sincerely appreciate it."

"I'm glad I could help," she said, her face spreading into a broad smile. "It's been nice talking with both of you. And, Jim…"

"Yes?"

"I want you to know my door is always open to you—professionally and otherwise. I think you're an interesting individual."

"Thank you," Snow said.

"It's not necessarily important to be successful in order to be interesting," Dr. Gilmore said.

CHAPTER 26

"Can you believe the way she was coming on to you?" Alice said.

Alice and Snow walked side by side down the sidewalk leading to the Sonata.

"What are you talking about?" Snow said. "Patronizing, more like. She's the kind of woman who enjoys grinding men up and leaving them by the side of the road like a pile of gravel."

"She was testing you," Alice said. "You passed. Apparently you're the type she's looking for. She must be tired of the stuffed shirts she usually meets. Probably has a secret craving for an untamed, rough-cut stallion."

Snow shook his head. "I've been there before. By the third date, she'd have me eating out of a dog dish."

They stopped at the end of the sidewalk, next to the Sonata.

Snow turned and looked at the house. "I'll bet she hasn't got one male patient."

Alice grinned. "You'd be surprised, Jim. Not all men are like you."

Snow nodded. "Yeah," he said. "I forgot about the S&M crowd."

A late-model Mustang pulled to a stop behind Snow's Hyundai. The driver's door opened and an attractive Asian with flowing, bleached blonde hair hopped out. She wore a tight-fitting red miniskirt with black heels. Her nails were long and glossy red.

Throwing her hair back behind her as she scampered up to the sidewalk and rushed toward Alice and Snow, she smiled happily.

Snow noticed her hands appeared quite large for her small size. Her ears seemed a little out of proportion also.

"Were you in to see Dr. Gilmore just now?" she asked. Her voice was rough, like that of a seventy-year-old chain smoker.

Snow nodded. "We just finished up."

"Isn't she wonderful?" she said, throwing her hair back over the opposite shoulder with a hand that Snow couldn't take his eyes off of. "I just love her. She has done so much for me. Made me whole again. I never thought it would be possible."

Snow arched his eyebrows. "Yes, it's good to be whole."

She wiggled her fingers at them.

"Have a beautiful afternoon," she said. Then she sashayed up the sidewalk to the front door. She opened it and stepped inside.

"Jesus," Snow muttered. "Look what that doctor did to that poor bastard. Turned him into a woman."

Alice put her hands on her hips and shook her head. "I sincerely doubt that. You know what I think? I think it bothers you to know that a person like her can be so happy, while you muddle along, trying to figure out what to do with your life."

"Just reporting an observation," Snow argued. "Frankly, I'm quite happy for her. But I do find it amazing. I just wonder, in this challenging economic environment, where someone such as her would be employed. Only one occupation comes to mind, and it's not legal in Las Vegas. Anyway…now what? What's our next move?"

Alice shook her head. "I don't know. You tell me."

"You seem agitated," Snow said. "Something bothering you that a good smack upside the head won't cure? Go ahead. Give it your best shot. I can take it. I've got a bottle of aspirin in the car."

"I can see I'll never hear the end of this," Alice said. "I should have kept my mouth shut."

"No," Snow said. "It's good to know how my partner feels about me. Tell you what—maybe we should just go our separate ways. You can run things the way you want. Find a partner with your level of enthusiasm, who dresses nice and can tap dance. Or just go it alone."

"Go it alone?" she snapped. "How far do you think I'd get on my own? I hate to admit it, but I actually do need you, Jim. How many people would be interested in hiring a black woman to investigate for them, when they could get a tall, capable-looking white guy? I need you for marketing purposes. You don't have to do anything. Just take it easy. I'll do all the legwork. All you have to do is walk around a little bit—and pretend that you give a shit!"

Snow said nothing. They stood staring at each other.

From his front jeans pocket, Snow's cell phone chirped.

He pulled it out, flipped it open, and put it to his ear. "Yeah, Jack. What's up?"

"Good afternoon, Jim," Jack Roberts said. "How are you and Alice this fine afternoon?"

"We're good, Jack," Snow said. "You sound cheerful. What's the cause of that?"

Roberts chuckled. "Kevin and I have been sitting here in his living room, having a nice chat. I believe we've come to a resolution of our conflict, finally."

"That's good," Snow said. "I'm glad to hear it."

Snow could hear Roberts breathing faintly into the phone, and then he spoke again, his voice even. "I'm wondering if you and Alice could join us for this discussion. I believe it may be of interest to you."

"Alright," Snow said. "We can leave now. Probably get there in twenty minutes. How does that sound?"

"Twenty minutes…hmm…that could be a problem…"

Snow frowned at Alice. "Why would that be a problem, Jack?"

Roberts sighed. "Well, you see, Jim. I've already been sitting here holding this gun for quite some time. It's beginning to feel a little bit heavy. I'm not sure I'll feel like hanging on to it for another twenty minutes. I may just go ahead and pull the trigger."

Snow's eyes widened. He stopped breathing. "Jack, what the fuck!" he rasped into the phone.

Roberts chuckled again. "Just hurry and get your worthless ass over here, Jim Snow. And don't even think about calling the police. If I get any indication at all that they're out there—I'll just go ahead and pull the trigger. Now don't say another word, or I'll put one right through this young fellow's heart. Just get the hell over here, fast."

"Alright," Snow said.

"Jim," Roberts said with glee. "That was another word." He hesitated and yelled, "*Bang!*" Then he laughed.

Snow disconnected the call. He speed-dialed Duke Ellis.

It rang four times before he picked up.

"Yeah, Jimbo," he said, his voice groggy.

"Duke!" Snow bellowed into the phone. "What the fuck is going on over there?"

He heard the sounds of Ellis stumbling around, along with heavy breathing.

"Oh, Jesus Christ!" Ellis said.

"What?"

"Jack Roberts's car is parked in Miller's driveway. And he's not in it."

"I know that," Snow snapped. "He's in the goddamn house with a gun pointed at Miller!"

"How do you know that?" Duke said.

"Because the bastard called me just now and told me, you dumb sonofabitch!"

"Fuck," Ellis muttered.

"What the hell happened?"

"I'm not going to lie to you, Jimbo," Ellis said. "I had the watch, while Sally was sleeping. Doc's had me on some new blood pressure medicine—beta blockers. Those damn things make me drowsy as hell. I fell asleep."

"Shit," Snow said.

"Yeah," Ellis said. "No doubt Miller already did that. Okay. Not to worry. Sally and I are saddling up. Locked and loaded. We're going in."

"Just don't do anything stupid, Duke," Snow said.

"No problem," Duke said. "We'll try to wait for you to get here—to handle that aspect."

Snow snapped the phone shut and shoved it into his front pocket. Alice was already in the car, checking the clip on her nine-millimeter.

He jogged around to the driver's side, slid in behind the wheel of the Sonata, and fired up the engine.

CHAPTER 27

With emergency flashers activated, Snow drove at a speed ten miles over the limit, easing through red lights where there was no traffic. Hoping against being pulled over by a Metro patrol officer.

Arriving at Kevin Miller's home, Alice and Snow surveyed the area in front of the house. There was no one around.

Snow skidded to a stop in the driveway next to Jack Roberts's Thunderbird. He set the brake and killed the engine.

Turning to Alice, he said, "It looks like Duke and Sally are inside. Here's the plan: you take the front door, and I'll slip around to the back—"

"And do what?" Alice snapped. "Throw rocks at him? You don't have a gun, Jim!"

Snow nodded. "That's a problem alright. You don't have an extra?"

"No." She stared at him with wide eyes.

"Alright. I'll admit it—that's a problem. We'll just have to make do. You go to the front door and wait there. Make sure your cell phone is on; set it to vibrate so it doesn't ring. After I get around back, I'll try to see whatever I can and call you. Okay?"

Alice nodded.

They climbed out of the Sonata, easing the doors shut. Alice walked briskly yet silently toward the front door, while Snow crept along the side of the house to the wooden gate.

He pushed down on the gate latch. It wouldn't budge. *Miller must have locked it*, he thought.

Snow stepped back from the fence, glancing around and looking for anything he might use to climb over the fence.

There was nothing.

"Jesus," he whispered under his breath.

He trotted around the front of the neighboring house to the front door, rang the doorbell, and waited.

A few moments later, a teenage girl opened the door. She appeared to be about sixteen, with disheveled, shoulder-length, brown hair. She wore white short shorts and a green top. It was inside-out, and her feet were bare.

Snow glanced past her into the living room. On the couch sat a teenage boy with tousled blond hair. He wore plaid shorts that seemed to be too big for Shaquille O'Neal. His T-shirt was backwards, and his sneakers lay on their sides under the coffee table. He sat grinning stupidly at Snow.

Snow wondered briefly what had been going on in there.

"Can I help you?" the girl said, smiling.

Snow pulled out his wallet, opened it, and displayed his Nevada private investigator license. The girl looked at it with big eyes.

"Oh," she said. "Are you a police officer? We haven't been doing anything wrong."

"No," Snow said. "I'm a private detective. I don't care what you've been doing. I have an emergency, and I need to get into the yard next door. Do you have a step ladder I can use?"

The girl's eyes went from the license to Snow. They were red and dilated. Her smile remained transfixed as she stared at him in wonder.

"There's one in the garage," she said. "Actually there are two: a tall one and a short one. You're welcome to use either one—if you like."

"Thank you," Snow said. "I appreciate it. May I come in?"

"Certainly," she said. And she stepped unsteadily away from the doorway.

Snow rushed past her into the living room toward the young man on the couch. He was suddenly overcome by the acrid smell of a controlled substance.

The boy on the couch remained frozen in place, grinning. "How's it going?"

"Fine," Snow lied.

"We were just watching TV," the boy said.

Snow glanced at the flat-panel TV sitting on a stand in front of the wall. It was off. He turned his head back toward the boy. "Where's the door to the garage?"

The boy turned and pointed toward it. "You need any help?" he asked.

Snow gave a quick look at the young girl. She was still standing at the front door. It was wide open, the doorknob still in her hand, the smile frozen on her face.

To the boy, Snow said, "Thanks, I can handle it. You two stay inside and continue watching television. Don't come outside."

"Awesome," the kid said.

In the garage, Snow found a six-foot aluminum ladder with spots of white paint scattered all over it. He carried it to the backyard, opened it, and set it next to the fence bordering Miller's backyard.

He raised his head slowly and peered over the top of the fence. The backyard was covered with Bermuda grass, bordered by gravel and bushes along the fence. In front of the patio door was a rounded slab of cement with lawn chairs, a glass table, and a gas grill.

Snow noticed the glass patio door, and the blinds were open. He would have to be quiet.

Then the realization struck him that he would need another ladder to climb down the other side of the fence.

He went back into the house and found the teenagers sitting together on the couch, staring at the television. It was still off. As he entered through the patio door, they turned to grin at him.

"How's it going?" the boy asked.

"Good," Snow said. "I'll need the other ladder."

"You need any help?" the boy asked.

"Thanks," Snow said. "I can handle it. Be sure to stay inside."

There was no reply from them. They watched like two cats as Snow crossed to the door that led to the garage.

A few minutes later, he emerged with the eight-foot ladder. He carried it out to the backyard, opened it, lifted it over the fence, and set it on the other side. He then climbed the short ladder, stepped over onto the taller ladder, and then down onto the grass.

Silently, he crept across the yard to the patio door. He stopped next to the edge of the closed screen door, tilted his head, and peered into the living room.

Inside, he saw Jack Roberts sitting comfortably in the middle of the sofa, his hands resting on his lap, holding a .38 caliber revolver with the hammer back. It was aimed at the chest of Kevin Miller, who stood across from him, perfectly still, his eyes wide, his face drained of all color.

To the left of Miller, Duke Ellis and Sally stood with their revolvers pointed at Roberts. No one spoke.

Snow moved away from the screen door and speed-dialed Alice on his cell phone.

She answered on the first ring. "What the hell is going on back there?" Alice whispered vehemently.

"The gate was locked," Snow whispered back. I had to get ladders from next door to get over the fence."

"What's happening inside?" Alice said.

"It's a standoff," Snow said. "Roberts has a gun pointed at Miller. Duke and Sally have Roberts covered with their weapons."

"What shall I do?" Alice said.

Snow thought for a moment. "Ring the front doorbell," he said.

"What?"

"Ring the doorbell. See what happens."

"What do you think will happen?" Alice snapped. "Someone will answer it. Is that the best idea you can come up with?"

"What do you want to do?" Snow argued. "Shoot the door-knob off?"

"Alright, alright," Alice said. "What are you going to do?"

"I'm going to watch," Snow said.

"You can't be serious."

"If something goes wrong, I can call the police."

"My hero," Alice said. "Alright, let me know when you're ready."

"Go ahead," Snow said, and then he tiptoed back to the patio door.

Inside, he heard the doorbell ring.

Without moving his eyes from Miller, Roberts said, "Go see who it is, but don't open it unless I tell you to."

Duke kept his gun aimed at Roberts while Sally went to the door. "It's Alice James!" she hollered back.

"What about Jim Snow? Is he with her?" Roberts yelled to her.

A moment later, Sally hollered back, "Yes. He's with her."

"Look through the peephole and make sure they're alone!" Roberts yelled.

"For chrissake, I did already!" Sally hollered.

"Alright. Let them in!" Roberts yelled.

Sally and Alice moved slowly into view, Sally with her revolver, Alice with her nine-millimeter aimed at Roberts.

"Where the hell is Snow?" Roberts demanded.

The latch on the screen door was broken. Snow slid it open and stood in full view. "You want snow—move to Minnesota," he said.

"Get the fuck in here!" Roberts snapped.

Snow stepped inside, closing the screen door behind him. Then he took two more steps toward Miller and stopped.

"Well, this is good," Roberts said, keeping his eyes on Miller. "It looks like the remainder of my firing squad has arrived."

"What now?" Snow said.

"I shoot this sonofabitch, and the rest of you shoot me. Something for everyone." His eyes darted to Snow and back to Miller. "Where's your gun, Jim?"

"We're in a recession," Snow said. "We've had to cut back on expenses. What difference does it make? Three bullets will kill you just as quickly as four."

"I just thought you'd like to join in, Jim. I know you don't like me much. I'm sure it would give you pleasure to blow a hole in me."

"That's thoughtful of you," Snow said. "Why don't you give me your gun, and all four of us will shoot you?"

Roberts chuckled. "That's much better than your last joke. You got any more?"

"If I think of any, I'll let you know," Snow said.

He began to inch slowly toward Miller. Other than him, Snow realized he was the only one in the room with nothing to do. The thought struck him that he needed to feel useful.

Gaining speed with longer strides, in a moment he found himself standing directly in front of Kevin Miller, staring at the black hole in the barrel of Jack Roberts's .38. He couldn't be sure what had propelled him to this position. He hadn't given it sufficient thought to make an intelligent decision. But now he was here, and there was no stepping back.

"What the fuck are you doing?" Roberts said. "Get the hell out of the way, or I'll blow a hole in both of you."

"No you won't," Snow said. "I'm a weightlifter. My muscles are denser than normal. No doubt it might kill me, but the bullet won't pass though."

"How do you know that?" Roberts said.

"They did a study at Stanford," Snow lied. "They made a bunch of dummies out of soft plastic and shot holes in them."

Snow couldn't believe this last statement that came out of his mouth. It sounded stupid even to him. He also was amazed at the tranquility that passed over him as he stood waiting for the possibility of death. But suddenly he understood the reason for the serenity. He was in no danger. Neither was Jack Roberts. Snow knew this as if he'd lived this moment before.

"You're not going to shoot anybody," Snow told Roberts.

"How did you come to that conclusion?" Roberts asked.

"How long have you been sitting there with that gun aimed at Miller? Almost an hour? If you really wanted to shoot him, you would have already done it. If you really wanted to die, you would have pulled the trigger as soon as Duke and Sally walked in here and put their guns on you. I think you've been trying to work up the nerve and can't do it. And here's why: It's a bad idea. It's senseless. And you know it."

Snow hooked a thumb over his shoulder aimed at Miller. "This guy didn't kill your daughter. But you don't like him, so you'd like to believe that he did. But he didn't."

"Then who did?" Roberts said.

"Somebody else," Snow said.

"Who?"

"We're not going to tell you that because then you'd drive over to their residence and pull your gun on them."

"You don't have a clue," Roberts said.

"That may be true," Snow said. "But we're convinced Miller didn't do it."

"How can you be sure?"

"We can have him volunteer to take a lie detector test. If he passes, you'll know for sure he's innocent. If he fails—shoot him then."

Roberts said nothing. Snow knew he had momentum in his favor.

"Now this much I'm pretty sure of," Snow said. "No doubt you've done a lot of things in your life that have been eating at you. None of us in this room is perfect. We all screw up now and then as we try to get through this somewhat miserable existence.

"You think your life sucks, Jack? Look at me. Do I look like I'm having fun? Hell no. But I can't just give up and end it all. Look at all the great buffets I'd be missing out on. Someday I might fall in love again—or at least discover a new beer that's better than anything I've ever tasted. At that point I'll be glad I'm still alive to enjoy it."

"You've got to find yourself a good woman!" Sally suddenly blurted out. "That's all you need, Jack Roberts!"

Snow raised an eyebrow. "Right," he agreed.

"Just say the word, Jimbo," Duke added, "and we'll take him down. It's your call, buddy."

"For chrissake, don't shoot," Snow said. "He's got that thing cocked. It's a hair trigger. Somebody sneezes and that gun will discharge."

"Good thinking, Jimbo," Duke agreed.

"Now, here's what I'm thinking," Snow said, spreading his hands. "I'm sure you feel that you deserve to spend time in hell to serve penance for every rotten thing you've done in your life. But all the years you've spent living in Barstow should have accomplished that.

"I say, put everything that's past behind you. Move forward. I know you have doubts right now. You're probably wondering how you got yourself into this mess you're in right now. And that now there's no way out.

"But I'm here to tell you that isn't true. I'm about to offer you the opportunity of a lifetime. The chance to turn back the clock and have it over again. As if this never happened."

Roberts's eyes narrowed. "What are you talking about?"

Snow put his hands together, clasping them. "Here's the deal, Jack. Anybody in this room interested in pressing charges against Jack for this incident that's taking place right now?"

No one spoke.

"Anybody?" Snow said. "If so, speak up."

No one spoke.

"What about you, Kevin?" Snow asked. "You want to file a complaint against Jack?"

Snow heard a high-pitched squeak from behind him. "No sir. No way. I'd just as soon forget it. That's fine with me."

"Okay," Snow said. "Here's what we do, Jack. You release the hammer on that revolver, very gently. Set it on the coffee table with the muzzle facing away from everyone. You think you can drive okay?"

Roberts nodded. His eyes began to tear.

"After you put the gun down, I want you to get in your car and drive back to Barstow. Duke and Sally will follow you to make sure you do that. And they'll stay there with you until this investigation is complete.

"Not only will you pay us for our services that you contracted for, but you will also pay the complete bill for Duke and Sally. Kevin pays nothing. I think that's only fair."

Roberts's words were thick with emotion. "Why would you be willing to do this for me?" he said.

"Because we're all good people here, Jack," Snow said. "And if you're dead or in jail, Alice and I won't get paid."

Jack Roberts nodded. He stood up and smiled, tears running down his face.

Then he raised his aim above Snow's head.

The .38 bucked.

An instant later the room exploded with gunfire.

Roberts flew backwards, landing on his back, blood oozing out of him onto the carpet.

With the smell of cordite in the air, five sets of wide eyes stared at the lifeless body on the floor. Not a word was uttered for a moment.

Finally Jim Snow spoke up.

"Jesus," he muttered. "That didn't turn out too good."

CHAPTER 28

"It's hard to believe," Jim Snow said. "Our first major case, and we conclude it by shooting our own client."

He was sitting in Alice's office in his swivel chair near the end of her desk. Alice sat behind her desk, with Duke Ellis and Sally Hollister seated in the client chairs across from her.

"I take full responsibility for this," Ellis said. "It was my watch, and I fell asleep. Had I been awake, we would have intercepted him before he got to the front door."

"Ah, don't get down on yourself, Duke," Snow said. "These things happen. It never benefits anyone to assign blame. And if you'd have been awake and confronted him, he'd probably have shot you first."

"I've been thinking about it," Alice said. "All night last night, in fact. And if it had turned out differently, Kevin Miller would probably be dead." She turned her head to Snow. "I have to hand it to you. You saved his life, Jim. That took a lot of courage to step in front of that gun and try to talk Roberts down. I've never seen anything like it."

Snow took a sip from his commuter mug and shrugged. "It didn't take any guts," he said. "I never had time to think about it. If I had considered my options thoroughly, I probably would have stayed outside on the patio."

"And if you'd had your gun with you," Alice said, "there would have been four bullets in Roberts and one in Kevin Miller. I would say everything turned out for the best. Even though I'm having a tough time dealing with having to shoot someone."

"You're not alone, Alice," Ellis said. "It turns my stomach just thinking about it. But I have to say, there are a lot of things I have to do that I'm not crazy about."

Sally nodded. "Like getting out of bed most mornings." She cackled.

Ellis chuckled along with her and then turned his eyes toward Snow. "Jimbo, how much did you get in advance for this case?"

Snow looked at Alice.

"A thousand," she said. "Ten hours for the two of us."

Ellis grimaced. "Ouch. I learned a long time ago to ask for full payment up front. We let them pay what they want. But when the money's used up, the investigation comes to a halt—until they pony up more funds. I don't have time to be chasing clients around a small claims court. And if they end up in the graveyard—that's a tough place to try and send an invoice."

Alice nodded. "That's worth thinking about."

There was a knock at the front door.

Snow got up from his swivel chair. "Let's hope that's a new client," he said. "Otherwise, we'll be sitting here playing cards all day."

Snow walked through the lobby to the front door. He opened it and found Kevin Miller standing there, holding a bottle of bourbon with a yellow ribbon tied around it.

Miller smiled nervously. "Mr. Snow," he said, "I've come to thank you for what you did."

He presented the bottle, and Snow took it from him, turning it in his hands, reading the label. "Old Whiskey River," he said. "Never heard of this—nice looking bottle. Thanks."

"It's not much," Miller said. "I didn't know what else to get, and I wanted to stop by to thank you—so I picked that up on the way."

He stuck his hand out. Snow shook it.

Snow hooked his thumb in the direction of the back offices. "Why don't you come inside. We've got the rest of the gang in there. Maybe we can try this stuff out, see if it's any good."

Miller smiled and nodded. He followed Snow back to Alice's office. Everyone turned and smiled at Miller.

"I found this guy outside," Snow said. "He's got whiskey, so I invited him in." Snow raised the bottle in front of him, then set it on Alice's desk. "We don't have any ice, but we've got plastic cups in my office and plenty of mixer from the faucet."

Snow left the office and reappeared a minute later with a stack of clear plastic cups. He removed one from the stack and set the rest on the table. Then he unscrewed the cap from the bottle, poured two fingers, and handed the cup to Miller.

"Okay," Snow said. "The bar's open. Who's thirsty?"

Ellis nodded. Sally and Alice screwed their faces up in disgust.

"It's not even ten o'clock," Alice said.

"You couldn't pour that stuff down my throat if I were drunk," Sally added.

Snow poured two more cups, gave one to Ellis, and kept one for himself. The three of them touched cups.

"Here's to the living," Snow said.

The three men drank.

"Smooth," Snow said. "Flavorful."

"Just enough bite," Ellis said. He took another sip and set the cup on the desk, exhaling loudly. "You know what this reminds me of?" He looked around the office. "*The Wizard of Oz*. At the end of the movie, when Dorothy was lying in bed and everybody showed up at the same time. Except nobody brought any whiskey."

"Which one of us is Dorothy?" Sally asked.

"Jim," Ellis said. "Jim is Dorothy." He chuckled and reached for his cup. "Pour more whiskey, Dorothy. Please."

Grinning, Snow unscrewed the cap and poured. "Glad to oblige, Scarecrow."

He poured more for Miller and then himself. Setting the bottle back on the desk, Snow leaned back in his chair, with his cup resting on his thigh. "Alright," he said. "Now let's get the whole story. Starting from the beginning—what the hell happened yesterday?"

"I can't say," Ellis declared. "I was watching the inside of my eyelids at the time."

Miller took a sip of his drink and cleared his throat. "Well, the doorbell rang. I went to answer it, thinking it was Duke wanting to use the bathroom again."

"Our black water tank is full," Ellis explained. "You can't just dump that thing into a storm drain."

"I thought you were just kidding when you mentioned using a five-gallon bucket," Alice said.

Sally cackled.

"Anyway," Miller continued, "I was getting ready to open the door. I had my hand on the deadbolt, looked through the peephole, and saw Jack standing there. I guess he heard me because he told me if I didn't open it, he'd shoot me through the door. So I opened it.

"We went into the living room. He sat down and called Jim. A few minutes later, the doorbell rang again. It was Duke and Sally."

"That's right," Duke said. "Jack was standing behind Kevin with his gun in his back. So we all went into the living room and stood there staring at Jack with our guns pointed at him, until reinforcements arrived."

"I was sure he would shoot me," Miller said.

"Why?" Alice asked.

"Because he was cheerful. As long as I've known him, I've never seen him happy about anything. When I saw how happy he was, I realized he was looking forward to dying—and taking me with him."

Snow's eyes narrowed. "That's right," he said. "I never thought of that. He was laughing on the phone. I was convinced what he was doing was just a cry for help. I guess I'm fortunate not to be dead."

"You would have been," Alice said. "He changed his mind at the last minute and decided to spare you. He must have liked your dumb jokes."

Snow nodded. "I think you're right, Alice. Looks like I got lucky again."

"I'm hesitant to ask, but what was the other time?"

"One incident that comes readily to mind," Snow said, "was the time I tried to clean the gas burners on my stove with carburetor cleaner. It would have been okay—except I forgot about the pilot light. I couldn't believe the house didn't start on fire. And it was a good learning experience. Now I know what it's like inside a combustion chamber when the spark ignites."

"I got you beat, Jimbo," Ellis said. "I blew a fuse one time. It was pitch dark in there, and I didn't have a flashlight, or even a match." He took a sip of whiskey. "You know how when you're replacing a spark plug and can't see the hole it screws into—you have to feel around with your fingers while you're holding the spark plug in the same hand. And you find the hole, but to be sure, you stick a finger in it?"

Snow nodded, grinning.

"I wasn't thinking," Ellis said. "Just a creature of habit, feeling around in the dark for the fuse socket. I think my head lit up for an instant, till I could get my finger back out of there."

Sally looked at Alice and shook her head.

There was a loud pounding at the front door.

The room got silent for a moment.

"Good God, who was that?" Ellis said. "Godzilla?"

"I think it's somebody knocking down a wall next door," Sally said.

It came again. Louder.

Snow got up and went to answer it. He opened the door to find a stout woman in her mid-seventies. She wore black jeans, black cowboy boots, and a black Western shirt with silver pinstripes. Her gray hair was pulled back into a ponytail, held in place with a rubber band. She was homely. Her nose looked familiar. Snow thought she resembled a female version of Johnny Cash. An instant before she spoke, he realized who she was.

"I'm Elaine Roberts from Bakersfield," she said. "I'm here to discuss the death of my son."

Snow looked her up and down.

"Don't worry," she said. "I don't have a gun with me. Are you Jim Snow?"

"Yes, I am," Snow said. "Why don't you come on in?"

She gave him a hard look. "Because you're standing in the doorway," she said.

Snow stepped aside, and she brushed past him. She kept walking, her boot soles striking loudly on the laminate floor.

"Turn right at the hallway," Snow said, following behind.

She entered the office and stopped just inside the doorway next to Kevin Miller. She put her hands on her hips and looked around the room.

Standing behind her, Snow announced, "This is Elaine Roberts from Bakersfield. She's Jack's mother." He was relieved to notice the bourbon bottle and cups were gone from the top of Alice's desk.

Ellis and Sally immediately stood up. Their eyes fixed on the woman, they stepped behind their chairs.

"Why don't you have a seat, ma'am?" Ellis offered. He shifted his eyes toward Jim, his eyebrows arched. "Jimbo, we've got to get on down the road. Need to get our tanks dumped. We thank you for your hospitality."

"Alice," Sally said, "I'll give you call. I want you to bring Jim with you to dinner one night next week."

Alice smiled and nodded.

"We'll grill some steaks," Ellis said.

"I'll bring the beer," Snow volunteered.

"Long as it's not that Chinese stuff," Ellis said.

Handshakes and hugs, and they were gone.

Elaine Roberts turned and looked at Miller. "Good to see you again, Kevin," she said. "Too bad it has to be circumstances such as these."

Miller nodded and bit his lip. "I'm sorry for your loss, Ms. Roberts. Sorry about what happened."

"Well, you're not the one who should be sorry," Elaine said. She paused and briefly looked around. "I'm going to sit down if nobody has an objection." She started moving toward the closest chair and lowered herself slowly into it.

"I'd better be taking off too," Miller said.

"Thanks for stopping by," Snow said.

Miller gave a wave and rushed out of the room. A few moments later they heard the front door open and shut behind him.

"Can I get you anything to drink, Ms. Roberts?" Snow asked.

She turned her head to him. "What do you have?"

"There's a coffee machine in the lobby. I could make a pot. We have water. Unfortunately, it's from the tap—we keep forgetting to pick up bottled water and other stuff."

"Oh," she said. "You don't keep anything harder than that in your office?"

"I could run and pick something up," Snow said. "There's a liquor store a little over a mile from here…"

She waved him off. "No. Forget about it. I don't want to make any trouble."

"It's no trouble," Alice said. "What would you like?"

"Bourbon," she said. "Just straight bourbon. No ice. I don't need ice. I don't like diluting my drinks."

Alice slid her bottom desk drawer open. She reached inside, gripped the bottle of whiskey around the neck, and set it on the desk with a resounding thud. Then she brought out a plastic cup and set that on the desk next to the bottle.

Elaine gave Snow a sidelong look, shifted it to Alice, and then to the bottle of whiskey.

"Old school," she said. "I like it. This is the way a private eye firm should be run."

Alice poured a small amount into the cup and set the bottle back on the desk.

Elaine Roberts stared at the cup. "That's not even enough to bother with," she said. "I'll be happy to pay for it, if you want?"

Alice poured more.

"You two aren't having any?" she said.

"I'm not much of a drinker," Alice said. "Jim?" She looked at him with raised eyebrows.

"Sure," Snow said. "What the hell."

Alice got an extra cup out. Snow poured it. He raised his glass to Elaine. She ignored the toast and drank hers down in one gulp, and then she set the cup back on the desk.

"Mind if I have another?" she said.

Alice poured it. She gulped that one down and set the cup on the desk.

"Would you like another?" Alice asked.

Elaine pursed her lips and exhaled. She shook her head. "That's my allowance for the day. My chauffeur is off today, and I hate lying to my doctor about my intake. That does hit the spot though, I must say. Thank you. I was up early this morning, and I always tend to drink too much coffee when I'm on the road. When that happens, I need to counteract the caffeine with a little something to even out my nervous system."

Snow took a sip of bourbon and sat down in his swivel chair. He held the cup in his lap with both hands. He leveled his gaze at the woman. "Ms. Roberts, Alice and I would like express our deepest regrets for what happened to your son. We—"

Elaine raised her hand. "That isn't necessary. First of all, call me Elaine. I don't like being formal, and I come from a long line of straight-talking folk. Now, I've been to the police station, and they told me, in detail, what happened. They let me read the police report—and I have to tell you it doesn't surprise me one bit." She sighed and looked at her empty cup. "I think I could use a little water, if you don't mind."

Alice reached for the handle of the desk drawer to get a fresh cup. Elaine raised her hand again. "I don't need a clean cup," she said. "No sense wasting the one I got—you can use that. I don't mind."

Snow got up. He left the room with the cup and came back a minute later with it full of water. He set it in front of her and sat down.

Elaine drank some water, set it back down, and cleared her throat. Her eyes were beginning to dampen. She straightened in her chair and continued. "I sincerely believe," she said, "that my son hired you to kill him. Maybe not consciously, but deep down inside his mind somewhere, I think that was the plan." She hesitated and looked down at her hands, folded in her lap.

Her eyes welling up, Alice pressed her lips firmly together and watched Elaine struggling with her composure. She said nothing.

Snow felt his throat constricting. He sipped more whiskey to help open it up.

Elaine Roberts raised her head up and met Alice's gaze. A tear slid down Alice's cheek. She opened a drawer, removed a tissue from the box inside it, and dabbed at her cheek.

"I don't want you to feel bad, missy," Elaine said. "You did the right thing. Had I been there, I'd have shot him myself." She took another drink of water. "I have to say, I'm not very proud of my son. I never have been. He was always a big pain in my behind. Now that he's gone on to meet his maker—I surely hope He has less trouble with Jack than I did.

"I don't think anyone was ever able to figure out the cause of it, but Jack always had a death wish. When he was twelve, he was seen sitting on the railing of an overpass, looking down at the traffic below. Trying to get up the guts to jump. A passing motorist went to a pay phone and called the police. They grabbed him and took him to the station. Several months of counseling followed that episode. We were told he was cured. The counselor told us he was just looking at life the wrong way, and he'd convinced him to look at the bright side."

She shook her head and took a sip of water. "When he was fifteen, he stood on the railroad tracks in front of an oncoming train. At the last minute, he jumped out of the way. The police were called. They took him down to the station. More counseling.

"My husband and I, rest his soul, started to think Jack might be homo." She raised her hands in front of her. "Now, I don't have anything against that lifestyle, but I do realize a lot of inner turmoil is created in some of those people when they can't properly deal with their lot in life and just get on with it the way normal homosexuals do."

Elaine let her hands fall back into her lap. "It wasn't long after that, Jack started showing an interest in girls and female pornography, so we realized his problem lay somewhere else.

"He tried, without success, many more times to do himself in. Always with the same result—failure. Eventually we stopped worrying about it. It was obvious his survival instinct was too strong—and now this. I think he finally figured out a way to get it done."

She leaned back in her chair. "But here's what else I think, and this is concerning the death of my granddaughter: I'm afraid Jack might have been the one who killed her. I realize Laura had her flaws, and I also know Jack wasn't happy with the way she turned out..."

"You think he might have intended it as a murder-suicide?" Alice said.

Elaine nodded. "I think that is a definite possibility. I think he may have killed her and then couldn't get up the guts to kill himself—so he took her out into the desert and burned up her body to destroy the evidence. Then hired you two."

"But he had a gun," Alice said. "Why not just shoot her, if he wanted her dead?"

"I thought about that," Elaine said. "I think it's possible he'd built up a lot of rage toward that girl. And he decided to let it all out—with a baseball bat." She put her hands up in front of her. "Now, maybe I'm wrong. And I hope I am. Maybe somebody else murdered Laura. That's what I want you two to find out for me."

"You'd like us to continue the investigation?" Snow asked.

"How much will it cost me?" she said.

"For one investigator, it's sixty an hour, plus expenses. If we work together as a team, which we prefer, it's a hundred an hour for both of us."

"Okay," she said. "That's fair. I'll take the both of you. Now, I'm willing to pay whatever Jack owed you for the time you've spent up until now—along with whatever it takes to find out who murdered my granddaughter. I'm an old woman. I know I won't live a lot longer, but I don't want to spend my last years fretting and wondering as to what happened with Laura. I want to know so I can mourn properly and set it to the back of my mind. Alright?"

Alice and Snow nodded.

"Any information you need," Elaine said, "I'll be happy to give it to you. I'm planning to stay in Vegas until after the funeral. I intend to mourn for my son in a practical way—shoot some craps and see a few shows."

CHAPTER 29

"Jack's Market."

"Good morning," Snow said. "May I speak to the manager?"

They were sitting in Alice's office, hunched over her speakerphone.

The voice sounded like that of a young man, rushed and impatient. "He's not here."

"Do you know what time he'll be in?"

"No," he said. "He's in Vegas. He may not be back for days."

Snow raised his eyebrows and looked at Alice. Into the phone, he said, "Is that Jack Roberts you're talking about?"

"Yeah—just a second."

They heard the sound of conversation in the background. Then the young man came back on the line. "Yeah," he said. "Jack Roberts. He's the owner. He's been in Vegas since last Wednesday. His daughter died. So he went there to deal with it. I haven't heard from him in a couple days. I don't know when he'll be back."

"Is there an assistant manager?" Snow asked.

The young man chuckled. "Are you kidding? Whaddya think this is, Kmart?"

"Who's running the store?"

"Nobody," he said. "Other than Jack, there are only two of us who work here. And while he's gone, we're both working twelve-hour shifts."

"Sounds like you're open twenty-four hours," Snow said.

"You're good with story problems," he said. "What is it you need? Maybe I can help you." He laughed.

"My name is Jim Snow. My partner, Alice James, is listening in. We're private investigators in Las Vegas. Who are we speaking with?"

"Really," he said. "That's cool. My name is Ricky. Ricky Oberender."

"Well, Ricky," Snow said, "it sounds as though you haven't heard about your boss…"

"What about him?" Ricky said.

"I'm sorry to have to tell you this, Ricky—but Jack Roberts is dead."

Silence. Snow waited.

"Ricky?"

"He's dead? Holy shit! What, was he in a car accident or something?"

"He was shot," Snow said.

"Who shot him?"

"We did," Snow said.

More silence.

"Ricky?"

"Damn!" Ricky said, his voice quivering. "Why are you calling here?"

"We just need to ask you some questions, Ricky," Snow said. "Do you mind?"

"I don't know," he said, his voice rising an octave. "I don't know anything."

"You don't know anything about what, Ricky?"

"What Jack was involved in," he said. "Whatever it was that got him killed. I just work here."

"You've got it all wrong, Ricky," Snow said. "Alice James and I were hired to investigate the murder of Jack's daughter. In fact, it was Jack who hired us."

"And you shot him? What was that all about?"

"It's a long story, Ricky," Snow said. "I'd rather not go into that right now."

"And now he's dead. So why are you still investigating if the guy who hired you is dead?"

"After we shot him, his mother hired us," Snow said.

Ricky's voice was frantic, his words shooting out like machine gun fire. "No way—you expect me to believe a story like that? I don't know who you are or what you want from me, but I'm hanging up right now and calling the cops."

Alice leaned closer to the phone. Her voice even and calm, she said, "Ricky, this is Alice James speaking. I know all of this sounds bizarre to you. But it's more complicated than my associate made it sound. The reason we're calling is because Jack's mother asked us to continue our investigation into her granddaughter's murder—which probably has nothing to do with Jack's death. I think they're isolated events. But we need to ask you about Jack, if you don't mind. We need to try and determine where he was the evening his daughter was murdered."

"Oh." Ricky's voice began to settle down to its normal tone. "That was last Tuesday night, right?"

"That's correct," Alice said.

"He was working here," Ricky said. "From eight o'clock Tuesday morning until midnight."

"He worked a double shift that day?"

"That's right," Ricky said. "I know because he relieved me in the morning, and I relieved him at midnight."

"Did he usually work two shifts?"

"No. What happened was Hector Martinez called in sick. Jack tried to get in touch with me to take the shift, but I wasn't home. I was spending the night at my girlfriend's place. So he carried the shift. He was here until midnight."

"Okay," Alice said. "This Hector Martinez, can you give us his phone number? We'd like to call him just to verify what you told us."

"Sure," Ricky said. "No problem. But now what am I gonna do?"

"About what?"

"The store. Jack's dead. What do I do about the store?"

"I don't know," Alice said. "Isn't there someone you can call?"

"Who am I gonna call?" Ricky said. "Jack ran the place by himself. I don't know what to do. How are me and Hector gonna get paid?"

"I don't know what to tell you, Ricky," Alice said. "I imagine Jack's mother will want to take it over. Or she may at least be able to tell you what to do. Why don't you call her?"

"I don't have her phone number," Ricky said. "Can you give it to me?"

"I'm sorry, I can't give out information like that, but we'll call her and explain the situation and tell her you'd like her to call you."

Ricky's voice began to rise again. "What if she doesn't call me?"

"I can't advise you about that," Alice said. "But if it were me, I would just lock the store up and go home. Wait for someone to call you. It's possible you may need to look for another job."

"Shit," Ricky said. "There ain't no jobs in Barstow."

Alice sighed. "Well, whatever you do, Ricky—don't move to Detroit. I'll try to get Jack's mother to call you."

He thanked her, and she disconnected the call.

Alice sat back in her swivel chair and rotated it toward Jim. "That lets Jack Roberts off the hook."

"I'm sure he'll be relieved," Snow said. "Should help him to rest in peace. Who's left?"

Alice spread her hands. "Crystal Olson, Kevin Miller, or someone we haven't thought of."

Snow nodded. "I agree. Now here's the morning line, the way I see it: Kevin Miller, eleven-to-one; someone else, six-to-one; Crystal Olson, odds-on favorite."

"I like the six-to-one odds," Alice said. "That's the type of horse I'd like to bet on. But we can't investigate someone we can't think of."

"That makes sense to me," Snow said. "So, we focus on the heavy favorite—but at the same time it would be nice to able to scratch the long shot from the race. Less competition for our attention."

"That's true," Alice agreed. "My mind does tend to wander back to Kevin Miller periodically. The slight possibility that he could have done it bothers my concentration. But he doesn't have an alibi, so how do you suggest we cut his odds to zero?"

"Lie detector test," Snow suggested.

"You think he'll agree to that?"

"From what I know about him, I'm sure of it," Snow said. "Let's call and get his approval. While we're waiting for that to happen, I think we should have another talk with Erin Potter to find out why she lied to us about Crystal."

"Maybe she'll agree to a lie detector test."

"I think we'd have a better chance of convincing Crystal to take one."

"The way her mother watches over her," Alice said, "I doubt she'd approve of that."

CHAPTER 30

"Kevin, this is Alice James. Jim and I are calling to thank you again for the lovely gift you brought by our office. That was very thoughtful of you—but also, Jim and I came up with an idea we'd like to run by you."

"Sure," Miller said. "Glad to hear it."

"Well, we were just sitting here discussing the case—"

"I thought your investigation was terminated along with Jack Roberts."

"It was," Alice said. "But Jack's mother reopened it."

"Oh."

"Now, although you still fulfill the basic requirements to be considered a possible suspect—you did have means, motive, and opportunity—the motive part of the equation seems quite weak at this point. It's almost fragile enough to collapse the entire tripod."

"Oh, that's good to hear," Miller said.

"Yes, it is," Alice agreed. "And Jim and I are trying to come up with a way to simplify our investigation by crossing you off completely. We think the best way to accomplish that will be with a lie detector test. What do you think?"

There was silence for a moment. Finally Miller spoke. "I don't know. What if I flunk it even though I'm telling the truth?"

"Chances of that are slim," Alice insisted. "But if it were to happen, we would only be out the cost of the test. Lie detector test results can't be used in court, and we wouldn't be any more suspicious of you than we already are."

"I don't know," Miller said. "I find that hard to believe. I expect that if I flunked the test, you would begin to think I killed her. Besides, the homicide detectives don't think I need to take a lie detector test."

"Why not?"

"Mel Harris—he told me he's sure I'm innocent."

"What makes him so sure? Did he say?" Alice asked.

"Four years of experience as a homicide detective," Miller said.

"He told you that was the reason?"

"Yeah. And he said only the guilty need to take lie detector tests. For the innocent—it's a waste of time. I think that makes sense."

"So, you're not interested in taking a lie detector test?"

"That's correct."

CHAPTER 31

Erin Potter came to her door in shorts and a baggy T-shirt. She escorted them to her living room without saying a word. The three of them sat down.

Snow, sitting next to Alice on the couch, produced a smile. Then he crossed his legs and arms.

"We'll try to make this short, Erin," Alice said. "I imagine you have to get to work pretty soon."

"It's okay," she said. "I'm off today." She made no attempt to smile. Instead she narrowed her eyes, her lips open slightly.

"Oh," Alice said. "You're off Mondays and Tuesdays?"

"That's right," she said. "Same schedule Laura had."

Snow pulled his spiral notebook out of his back pocket and began to scribble.

"Right," Alice said. She leaned back and interlaced her fingers in her lap. "We wanted to check with you again about the bruise on Laura's jaw."

"Okay. What would you like to know that I didn't already tell you?" Her eyes narrowed even more.

"We need to double-check that. You said it was eight months ago, when Kevin Miller and Laura broke up the first time."

"That's right."

"And that's when Laura had the bruise. The day after."

She kept her eyes focused on Alice. "That's right."

"You're sure it wasn't five months ago—a few days after Easter?"

"I'm certain of it," she said evenly. "If someone told you it was in April, they're mistaken. It happened in January. The day she told him to leave."

"Also," Alice said, "you told us that Kevin backhanded Laura?"

"That's right."

"Which side of her face had the bruise?"

"Her left?"

"But Kevin Miller is right handed. If he backhanded her, the bruise would have been on the right side of her face."

"He must have used his left hand," Erin argued.

"I don't think that's likely," Alice said.

Erin shrugged. "I don't know if it is or not. I'm just telling you what Laura told me happened. She said he hit her with the back of his hand, and she told him to pack up and move out."

"And that was in January."

"That's correct."

"Erin," Alice said, "you say you're off Mondays and Tuesdays."

"That's right."

"You were off last Tuesday?"

"I was," she said.

"Would you mind telling us where you were from the middle of the afternoon that day until later that evening?"

"Of course not," Erin said. "I was with a friend. I went over to visit her around ten o'clock Tuesday morning, and I stayed until Wednesday morning."

"Do you mind if we check with her on that?"

"Of course not," she said. "Her name is Charity Lane. She lives not far from here. I'll get her address and phone number for you if you like. I'll even call her and tell her you're on your way over. I'm sure she's home. She's off today, and she never goes anywhere. She's a real homebody."

They were in the Sonata, fastening their seat belts.

"Jim," Alice said, "do you feel like this is a waste of time?"

"The entire investigation?" he said. "Or going to visit Charity Lane?" He slipped the key into the ignition and cranked the engine.

"Charity Lane," Alice said.

"Of course," Snow said. "Erin is probably on the phone right now, telling her what to say. Unless she actually *was* over there that night."

"What do you think?"

"I think Crystal found out about Andrew Tully and Laura, had it out with Laura, and hit her in the head with the baseball bat. Then she called her good friend Erin, begging for help disposing of the body. Erin drove over to Crystal's home and lent her a helping hand."

"Yes," Alice said. "That makes a nice theory. I think I can go along with that."

CHAPTER 32

Charity Lane lived in a two-story, three-bedroom home in the Spring Valley area of Las Vegas. A plump woman in her mid-twenties, she was of average height, with black hair cut to the middle of her ears. She had a bulbous nose, small eyes and mouth, and flat cheekbones. Her head was as round as a volleyball, and it rested on a short stump of a neck.

She came to her door smiling broadly, offered a handshake to Alice and Snow, and then led them into her dining room, where she seated them at a cherrywood dining table. A matching hutch stood against the wall; the other walls were adorned with framed paintings of various flowers.

"This is lovely," Alice said, studying the pictures.

"Thank you," Charity said. "I did all the paintings myself, including the ones in the living room—although those aren't flowers. I prefer painting flowers, but I didn't want them in every room."

"They look professionally done," Snow said, scooting his chair closer to the table. "Have you considered selling any of them?"

Charity stood at the head of the table, her hands resting on the back of her chair. "I do, actually," she said. "Though only to my customers. I'm a hairstylist. I converted one of my bedrooms upstairs. Had it plumbed for water and put in a shampoo sink, along with everything else I needed to turn it into a functional salon." Charity smiled politely and then asked, "Would you like some pie and coffee?"

Alice and Snow looked at each other. Alice turned her head back toward Charity. "Oh no, I don't think so, but thank you."

"Are you sure?" she said. "I have a refrigerator full of pies. There is nothing I love doing more than painting—except baking pies. I have cherry pie, blueberry, pumpkin, and banana cream."

"Banana cream sounds good," Snow chimed in.

Alice smiled. "Alright, I'll have the blueberry." She started to get up. "Let me help you with it."

Crystal put her hand out. "No, you relax, I'll get it. Anyone want cream or sugar?"

They shook their heads.

"Just cream in my pie," Snow said, grinning.

She brought out the pie and the coffee, and then she sat down.

Alice put her napkin on her lap and took a sip of coffee. "Did you grow up in Las Vegas, Charity?"

Charity began to cut a slice from her pumpkin pie with her fork. "No," she said. "I'm from Green River, Wyoming. It's a nice little town, but probably not a very good place to try to set up a beauty salon. I picked Las Vegas because it's not too far from home, so I can visit my folks on a regular basis. And I like it here. Plus, it's nice to know some of the water I use here flows past my hometown to get here."

"So, how did you meet Erin Potter?" Alice said.

Charity had finished carving through her slice of pie and slid her fork under it. "She's been a customer for a couple years now. One of my other customers recommended me to her." She lifted the forkful of pie to her mouth and began to chew.

"The two of you are close friends?" Alice asked.

She set her fork on her plate and wiped her mouth with her napkin. "No," she said. "The only time I see Erin is when she comes over to get her hair cut."

"Was she here last Tuesday?"

"No. The last time I saw Erin was about three weeks ago."

"Erin told us she was here most of the day and spent the night here," Alice said.

Charity put her hands in her lap and looked Alice in the eye. "I know. She called me not long before you got here. She wanted me to tell you that story, and I told her I would, but I can't lie about that."

"Why do you think she would need an alibi?" Alice said.

Charity shook her head. "I have no idea. Maybe she had something to do with that murder, but I doubt it. She doesn't seem like that sort of person—and I hope nothing I tell you here will get back to her or anyone else."

"We'll keep it to ourselves," Alice said. "What sort of person is Erin Potter?"

"She's the type who lies about nearly everything—like it's her hobby. She collects lies the way some people collect pressed flowers. Keeps them all filed away for easy access and brings them out whenever she can, to show everybody. I don't understand why she does it, but then, I don't understand why most people do the things they do."

She reached for her coffee cup, took a sip, and set it back on the table. "One thing that has remained consistent, though, is what happened to her parents. Apparently they both ended up in prison, and it sounds like their convictions had to do with her."

"When did they go to prison?" Snow asked.

"She was nine, I think," Charity said. "Her grandparents raised her."

"That's too bad," Snow said. "That could explain a lot."

Charity nodded. "Yes, it's sad. Also, she's had nothing but trouble with the men she's dated. I don't know where she meets these guys, but they're all losers. Well, I should talk. I've never gotten past a second date. I've met some on the Internet who wanted to meet me at a Starbucks. They walked up to me, took one look, and turned around and left. Without a word. Talk about rejection."

"I've heard worse stories," Snow said. "I knew a guy who would tell the women what they could expect he would be wearing. He always wore something different. He'd even comb his hair a different way. If he didn't like the way she looked when she walked in, he'd get up and leave without a word. If she looked okay, he'd tell her he spilled something on his clothes and had to change. And then there's the other side of it. I got into an e-mail exchange with a woman one time whose photos looked like Jennifer Lopez. She turned out to be a drag queen."

"I'm hoping the story ends there," Alice said.

Charity giggled.

Alice turned to her. "Charity, did you know Laura Roberts?"

"Yes," she said. "She was a regular also."

"What was your impression of her?"

"I would say that she was the Evel Knievel of intercourse. That was all she ever talked about. The way she talked, it sounded like she enjoyed the risk of getting caught."

"Getting caught how?"

"Any way possible. In public places. With strangers she'd just met."

"How about with someone's fiancé?"

"Is there anyone in particular you had in mind?" Charity asked.

"Andrew Tully."

"Crystal's fiancé."

"Do you know Crystal too?" Alice said.

"Yes," Charity said. "She's also a customer of mine. In answer to your question, I never heard anything about Laura and Andrew. That doesn't mean it didn't happen. That doesn't seem like something Laura would have wanted to divulge to me."

"What do you think of Crystal?" Alice said.

"I don't know what to think of Crystal," Charity said. "She hardly ever talks. When she does, it's usually just small talk. She keeps most of her thoughts to herself."

Snow had just finished chewing a mouthful of pie. He swallowed the last of it and reached for his coffee cup. "You've never socialized with any of these women?"

Charity shook her head. "I have a small number of close friends, but Erin and Crystal aren't included. Nor was Laura. They're not the sort I would be interested in getting together with."

"How do you know so much about them," Snow asked, "if all you do is style their hair?"

Charity smiled and sat back in her chair. "Most people, it seems, like to talk about themselves. When they encounter someone willing to listen, who shows a genuine interest in them—they'll tell you practically anything you're willing to hear. All you have to do is ask. And it doesn't seem like it's important how well they know you. As long as they feel comfortable with you."

"All of your customers are like that?" Snow said.

She nodded. "Pretty much. Except for the ones like Crystal. And I must say, she is the biggest mystery of all."

"It looks like your theory is beginning to show promise," Alice said, climbing into the passenger side of Snow's car.

"Yeah," Snow agreed. "What's the next step?"

Alice snapped her seatbelt into place. "I think we need to dig deeper into Crystal's past. See if we can find an old high school friend—one who doesn't have an aversion to telling the truth."

Snow slid into the driver's seat and shut his door. "Somebody like Charity," he said. "What a refreshing change that was. If I'd had any sense when I was younger, I would have married someone like her instead of the two beauty queens I got hitched up with. After the honeymoon, they all lose their looks anyway."

"Hmm," Alice said. "Maybe you'll begin to feel more strongly about me if I fill my refrigerator up with pies."

CHAPTER 33

"Hello. This is Holly."

"Holly Whitten?" Alice asked.

"Yes."

"Hi, Holly," Alice said. "This is Alice James and Jim Snow. We're on the speakerphone together."

"Oh, yes," Holly said. "How's the weather down there in Las Vegas?"

"It's heating up," Alice said.

"Oh, it's raining here."

"We get that too," Alice said. "For ten minutes every six months."

Holly laughed.

"So your softball game got rained out, then?"

"It's been raining all day," Holly said. "There was no doubt about that happening."

"I want to thank you for returning my message on Facebook."

"It's no problem," Holly said. "I'm glad to help out. Plus I was a little curious; you said this concerned Crystal Olson, right?"

"Yes, that's right."

"Is she in some sort of trouble?"

"No," Alice said. "We tend to cast a pretty wide net during our investigations so we don't miss anything."

"What sort of investigation is it?"

"It's a murder," Alice said.

"Oh!" Holly said. "That sounds interesting." She hesitated. "Well...unless...Crystal—did she know the victim very well?"

"Well," Alice said, "yes, she did. They were friends. And you said in your e-mail you and Crystal were friends in high school?"

"Yes," Holly said. "We were best buddies because of softball, and also we seemed to migrate toward each other."

"How so?"

"Crystal was very quiet and standoffish. And so was I. We weren't joiners. Other than softball, we never participated in any other activities in high school."

"Why was that?" Alice asked.

Holly sighed. "I think Crystal was just wired that way. But for me it was hard. My parents worked for a funeral home while my sister and I were growing up. They were both morticians—in fact, that was how they met. Eventually the owner retired, and my parents took the funeral home over from him, and my sister and I both went to work there too. After high school, we both got associate degrees in mortuary science. We're both licensed."

"So you're..."

"Yes," she said. "We're both morticians. My sister's a year older than me, so she started school first, and she liked it, so I went. We're a lot alike. And after my parents retire, we'll probably take over the business ourselves.

"You know, people think it's really gross working with dead people, but that's only because they're never around them at all. The only time they ever see one is at a funeral or a wake. But my sister and I grew up around the deceased. Every day.

It's no big deal when you've seen them on a regular basis from day one. And the great thing about it is, while you're working with them, since they're dead, they don't give you any trouble. And the family members are always subdued, so it's a very peaceful work environment. There's no stress involved. You may have noticed funeral directors are usually very calm and collected?"

"I have noticed that," Alice said.

"Well, of course they have to be that way to lend comfort to the family. But it's also because the family members are so depressed they hardly ever get on your case about anything."

"That's interesting," Alice said.

"But getting back to the original point I wanted to make," Holly said. "When people know you work in a funeral home—or even if it's only that your parents do—they don't want to be around you. They don't even want to touch you. So my sister and I couldn't get dates with anybody decent. The guy who took me to the senior prom had a face full of zits I couldn't bear to look at. And even *he* wouldn't kiss me goodnight when he got me home, which was right after the dance ended.

"And my sister and I still live at home with my parents. She's twenty-seven and I'm twenty-six. We'll probably end up old maids."

"That's too bad," Alice said.

"Yes, it is," Holly said. "But you know, I'm not going to give up a profession I love just so I can meet the standards of some guy. And I'm a firm believer in fate. Someday I'll meet my soul mate. And he won't care what I do for a living. He's out there somewhere, I can feel it."

"That's encouraging," Alice said. "Now, about Crystal. You said she had trouble getting along with people—"

"No," Holly said. "I didn't say that. I said she was standoffish. She was shy around people. I think she had a hard time relating to them. She had her own thing going on, and I also think she was easily frustrated by the things people say and do."

"I see. And how did she express that frustration?"

"She mostly just kept her mouth shut and kept it inside."

"Were there times when she didn't?"

Holly hesitated. "There were a few times when it came boiling out. One time, in school, she was passing another girl in the hallway. The girl insulted her. I don't even know what she said. Crystal spun around and pushed her really hard into some lockers. The girl hit her head and cut it a little."

"Was anything done about it?" Alice asked.

"One of the teachers who saw it happen took her by the arm and escorted her to the principal's office. He gave her a lecture and let her go back to class.

"The next incident was a little worse. This was in the hallway again. A couple of girls were running. One of them slipped and ran into Crystal. Knocked her over. She got back up and punched the girl in the eye. It swelled up quite a bit. So, back up to the principal's office with her again. Another lecture, and back to class. The girl got home, and her parents saw her swollen eye and called the police. They came out and talked to Crystal, but there were no charges because the other girl ran into her first. And they were just in high school.

"And the other time I remember, we were playing our toughest rival. There was a lot of bad blood between our schools. Not just in softball, but all sports. Crystal was batting. The pitcher threw one inside right at her. Hit her on the shoulder. Crystal got up with her bat and started walking toward the pitcher with it. She got halfway to the mound and threw the bat at her. It just barely missed the girl's head. She got suspended for a couple of games for unsportsmanlike conduct. But nobody even counseled her about it."

"What did you think about that?" Alice said.

"At that point," Holly said, "I thought she seriously needed to talk to somebody. I told her that. I told her parents that. She needed counseling. But they wouldn't listen to me. I mean, after that thing with the bat—I was afraid she was going to kill somebody someday."

CHAPTER 34

"These aren't bad," Snow said. "It's amazing that they got the entire print of the shoe for all three photos. Pretty good detail on the tread pattern."

Snow was sitting in his swivel chair next to Alice. They were staring at one of the shoe print photos from the crime scene on Alice's notebook computer.

"Who sent you these photos?" Snow asked.

"Mary from the lab."

"How much did that set us back?"

"Nothing," Alice said. "She's a friend of mine."

"It's incredible," Snow said, "the amount of information you get out of Metro. How many contacts do you have there, all total?"

"They're not contacts, Jim," Alice said. "They're friends. I have three in the crime lab, one at the coroner's office, two in Robbery, four in Homicide, one in Vice, one in Violent Crimes. And a few others scattered about in administrative jobs. How many do you have, Jim?"

"Maybe four and a half total," Snow said. "But I can't be sure. It's been a while. A lot of the people I worked with quit the force."

"You don't stay in touch?"

"Sure," Snow said. "But you know how it is—time marches past you. By the time you get around to giving them a call, some other person answers the phone—and they don't speak English. That's a pretty good indication they've moved."

"Or maybe they hired servants?" Alice said.

"Yeah," Snow said. "That'll be the day." He turned his eyes back to the monitor. "You just have the photos of the shoe prints?"

"No," Alice said. "Mary sent me the entire set from the crime scene."

"Anything worth looking at?"

"Other than the shoe prints, just the gas can."

"What was so special about the gas can?"

She closed the photo and brought up another photo. It showed the blackened corpse, with a stump of a baseball bat on top of the torso. Lying beside the body was a small rectangular can. Snow moved his head closer. Alice zoomed in on it.

"Hmm," Snow said. "That's not what I was expecting. When Mel told us it was a gas can, I thought it was the kind you use to fill a lawn mower."

"Right."

"But this looks like one of those quart-size cans that are used to fill camping lanterns and stoves. What do they call that fuel?"

"White gas," Alice said.

"Yeah, that's the stuff," Snow said. "Tell you what—why don't you print out the pictures. We can take them with us. I think we should take a run out to the crime scene. If those shoe prints are still visible, I'd like to take a look at them close up—in daylight."

212

A warm front had been moving into southern Nevada, driving the temperature higher. At shortly after nine a.m. as Snow pulled the Sonata onto the gravel shoulder of Stober Road, it was already over ninety degrees.

Alice and Snow climbed out of the Sonata and stood next to it scanning the barren landscape. Instead of a business suit, Alice wore a pair of brown cotton slacks with a white blouse. She slung her purse over her shoulder, clamping a file folder full of crime scene photos under her arm, and walked around the front of the car to the edge of the pavement.

"There's a lot of nothing out here," Snow said, squinting against the sunlight. "I can see why the perp picked this area. This road serves no purpose. Other than a place for young Johnny to run the family car through the quarter on Sunday afternoons."

"It looks like they planned for a subdivision to be built here during the housing boom," Alice said. "All they built were the roads."

They turned and looked at the blackened section of flat ground, sixty feet from the road, where the body had burned. It was all that remained. The crime scene had been abandoned, the yellow tape removed and discarded.

Alice and Snow split up, fanning out on both sides of the burned area. They walked along the perimeter checking the ground for anything that might have been overlooked, working their way inward. There was nothing to see, only portions of footprints assumed to be left by investigators and crime scene analysts. The ground was hard, with little dust covering it. Nearing the slight trail left by the dragged corpse, Snow came upon a small patch of dirt a couple of feet in diameter.

He squatted down and examined it. It appeared to be the same color and texture as the ground around it, but it looked as though it had been shaken out of a container and smoothed over.

Snow stood up and looked at Alice. Twenty feet closer to the burned spot on the other side of the trail, she stood bent over at the waist, staring down at the ground.

"Alice," Snow said, "I think I found something here. It looks like some dirt was dumped here and spread out to make it look like it's part of the landscape. I think one of the footprints might have been left here. It looks as though someone came along and evened it out with a stick or something."

Alice straightened up. "I've got the same thing here." She opened the file folder, slipped the three footprint photos out, and looked through them. She put one on top of the stack and examined it, comparing it to the patch of dirt in front of her.

"This is it," she said. "It's obvious from the arrangement of the rocks and the shape of the sagebrush next to it. The footprint was right in the middle of the dirt. You can't see it from the photos, but you're right. Somebody shook some dirt out here and stuck their foot into it. It was obviously staged. It's three feet from the trail. Why would they even step over here? If you're dragging a body out here, you're going to be in front of it, and the body will cover your tracks. Except when you're walking back to the car. Or more likely, running back."

"Not only that," Snow said, "but this ground is too hard. It's not conducive to yielding clear footprints. You can't see much of anything here."

They continued walking together on either side of the trail toward the burn area. Fifteen feet from it, Alice stopped, looking down.

"Here's the third one," she said. "Same thing. A patch of dirt sprinkled out in a circular area. This is definitely where it was, and now it's been graded flat. The footprint is gone."

Snow put his hands on his hips and shifted his gaze to Alice. "Why would somebody do that? Go to the trouble of putting dirt down to stage some footprints, and then come along later and remove them?"

"I don't know," Alice said. "Maybe the perp changed her mind and got nervous about the prints being traced to the shoes."

"I think you're right," Snow said. "This was clearly a woman who did this. She put on a pair of men's shoes and left distinct prints of the soles in dirt that she brought here with her. She planned this out pretty good."

"Where'd she get the men's shoes?" Alice said.

Snow considered this for a moment. "She bought them. If this was a crime of passion, which it probably was, after the murder she drove to a department store and bought a pair of men's work boots. That's why she went to the trouble of bringing the body out here instead of just burning the house down. She could make it look like a man killed her."

"Plus, she wouldn't have to sacrifice all her belongings and a perfectly good house."

"I don't think many houses in Vegas are perfectly good anymore," Snow countered. "Most of them are upside down; I think the owners would be happy to burn them down."

A rattling sound from the road caught Snow's attention. He turned his head toward it and saw a man with a floppy hat slowly pushing a grocery cart along the edge of the pavement. He had a bushy gray beard and wore faded jeans, a long-sleeve shirt, and tennis shoes with the backs flattened from walking on them. His cart was filled with clothes, a sleeping bag, and what appeared to be a rolled-up tent.

He stopped pushing the cart a short distance from the Sonata and turned his head toward Alice and Snow. Then he reached behind him with his left hand up under his shirt and scratched his back.

Snow looked at Alice. "You seen enough here, Alice?"

She nodded, and they walked back to the road.

As they approached, the homeless man pushed his grocery cart to a stop in front of them. He reached under his shirt and scratched his back again in the same spot. Then he looked at Snow.

"You folks need any help?" he said.

"No, we're fine," Snow said.

The old man nodded. He reached into his back pocket and pulled out a black comb. Holding it out in front of him, he asked, "Did you drop this?"

Snow smiled. "No, I didn't. But that looks like a really nice comb. You wouldn't want to sell it, would you?"

The old man shrugged. "I don't know. How much you want to pay for it?"

"How much you want for it?" Snow said.

The old man shrugged again. "Couple bucks?"

"I don't know," Snow said. "Looks like it's worth more than that."

"How much you offering?" the old man asked.

"I was thinking somewhere around forty," Snow said.

The old man's eyes widened. His mouth hung open. "Forty bucks?"

"Sure."

"Alright." The old man held it out to him.

Snow pulled his wallet out and produced two twenties. He looked at the comb. "The only problem," he said, "is that I already have a comb. I really don't need another one to carry with me."

The old man's eyes narrowed. "Oh."

"You spend much time on this road?" Snow asked.

"Every day I'm on it," the old man said. "At least once or twice, I like to walk it. It makes me feel like I'm going somewhere. Like I'm on vacation."

Snow chuckled. "Yeah, I know the feeling. Tell you what—you hang onto the comb. Keep it with you. If I happen to be driving by and need to comb my hair and discover that I've forgotten my comb, I can use that one. How about if I pay you another twenty for a carrying charge. Would you be agreeable to that arrangement?"

The old man's eyes widened again. "Oh, very agreeable," he said.

"Good." Snow slipped another twenty out of his wallet and handed the three bills to him.

The old man folded the bills in half and shoved them into his front pocket. "Anything else you need?" he said.

"No, I think that should do it," Snow said, smiling.

He and Alice walked toward the car.

Behind him, Snow heard the old man raise his voice slightly. "I noticed you folks were out looking at the burn spot."

Alice and Snow turned to look at him. "That's right. We were."

"Find what you were looking for?"

"Maybe," Snow said. "Why do you ask?"

"I take it you're investigating what happened here."

Snow nodded. "Yes, we are."

"In that case, you might be interested to know about what I've seen."

"And what would that be?"

"A little white car," the old man said. "Saw it driving by here quite a few times since that body burned up out there. I'd say at least once a day. Two women in it."

"That's interesting," Snow said. "A little white car with two women in it. Had you ever seen them before last week?"

"Nope," he said. "And I'll tell you something else interesting: after they took down the yellow tape and the police cleared out of here two days ago, those women stopped and got out of their little white car and walked out there to where the two of you were standing. They had a tire iron with them. And I saw them rubbing the ground with it. I was back the road a ways, but I could see what they were doing. I thought it was some kind of a goofy ritual or something. And after I thought about it, I figured they must have had something to do with that body being burned. They must have forgotten to cover something up. Kind of stupid, after the cops already left and finished investigating. But since you're still interested—I thought it might be useful to you."

"It is," Snow said. "Would you recognize the women if you saw them again?"

"No. They were too far away. All I could see was that they were short. Both the same size and figure. One looked older than the other."

"What about the car? Did you notice a make and model or license plate number?"

"No. It was small and white. Fairly new. That's all I could see from that far away."

"Okay," Snow said. "Is there anything else you can tell us before we go?"

"Yeah," the old man said. He looked up at the sky with his mouth hanging open. "I'd advise you to stay out of the sun." He turned his head back to Snow. "It can get pretty hot out here."

"Thanks," Snow said. "That's good advice."

"Have a pleasant morning, the both of you," he said. He scratched his back one more time and resumed pushing his grocery cart, the basket rattling as the wheels rumbled along over the rough asphalt.

Alice and Snow stood next to the car staring after him.

"He seems content," Alice observed.

"Yeah," Snow said. "Considering his situation—I wonder why."

"For one thing," Alice said, "he's completely free. For another, I imagine he has drastically lowered his level of expectation."

"Jesus," Snow muttered. "And here I thought mine had hit rock bottom."

"Those two women he saw fit the description of Kathy and Crystal Olson," Alice said. "Don't you think?"

"It sounds like it could be them."

"What about the car? Did you notice what type of car Crystal was driving?"

"A white Honda Accord," Snow said. "I even wrote it down. But that doesn't really mean much; there must be a hundred thousand little white cars registered in Clark County."

"True," Alice said. "But it looks like we're onto something with meat in it this time. I think I'll print out some photos of Crystal from her Facebook page. If we can find a pair of men's boots at a department store near Crystal's residence with soles that match the prints in the photos from the crime lab, we can ask the manager to check the footage from their security cameras. If we can place her at a store buying those boots a couple of hours before the fire—that's all we need."

CHAPTER 35

The closest department store to Crystal's residence was a Walmart located near West Charleston Boulevard. Alice and Snow stood in front of the racks containing the size twelve men's shoes, studying the soles of the various styles.

"It definitely wasn't a hiking shoe," Snow said. "The lugs on those are too pronounced. Tennis shoes have the wrong pattern."

Alice reached down and picked up a pair of brown high-top work boots. They resembled a hiking boot, but with a moderate tread on the outsole. She turned them over and examined the soles.

"What do you think of these?" she said.

Snow held out one of the photos of a shoe print taken at the crime scene. They looked at the photo, the boots, and back to the photo.

"It looks like we've got a match here," Snow said.

"Definitely a match," Alice agreed. "You got your tape measure?"

Snow set the stack of photo printouts on top of a pair of oxfords and dug into his pocket, pulling out a pocket-size eight-foot tape measure. While Alice held the boots, Snow measured one of the soles in both directions.

"Thirteen by five," he said, "give or take a sixteenth."

"Bingo," Alice said. "Thirteen by five. That's the measurements Mary gave me for the prints."

"And the width is measured across the toe, right?" Snow said.

"Of course," she said. "That's the widest part. She said the heel was four and a half."

Snow measured the heel. "Four and a half," he said. "Alright. Let's get 'em."

"Fantastic," Alice said.

They turned to leave and noticed a stocky Hispanic man staring at them with his mouth open.

"How's it going?" Snow said.

"Pretty good," the man replied.

As they walked away on their way to a checkout counter, Snow glanced over his shoulder at the man. He had picked out of pair of the same boots from the size eleven rack. He was turning them over in his hands like a kid with a newly opened present at Christmas.

After purchasing the boots, Alice and Snow waited near the cash register for the store manager. He arrived a few minutes later, and Snow introduced himself and Alice. He showed the manager his PI license and the boots.

"We're investigating a murder," Snow said. "We believe the perpetrator may have purchased these boots from this store between the hours of, say, three and seven p.m., a week ago Tuesday."

The store manager nodded. "Okay."

Alice held out three photo printouts of Crystal. "These are pictures of the woman we believe may have purchased the boots during that time. However, it's possible it might have been someone else."

"Okay," he said. "How can I help?"

"We would appreciate it very much," Alice said, "if you could go back through your security camera footage covering the time between three and seven p.m. Tuesday, September fourteenth, and see if the woman in these photos or anyone else bought a pair of these boots in a size twelve."

The store manager pulled out a pad of notepaper and a pen and scribbled. He looked at the tag on the work boots and scribbled some more. He put the pad of paper and pen back in his pocket. "Okay," he said.

Snow handed him his business card. "Call us, either one of us, at the cell phone numbers on this card as soon as you've checked. We need to know either way. Okay?"

The store manager smiled. "You got it," he said.

They shook hands all around and left the store.

To broaden the scope of their shoe investigation, Alice and Snow visited four other Walmarts. They were farther from Crystal's residence, but it was possible, they decided, that Crystal may have driven to a store further away, just in case someone figured out her plan—yet didn't feel like doing too much legwork.

After speaking with the store managers at those outlets, they returned to the office. While they waited, Alice searched the Web sites of other department stores, such as Kmart and

Kohl's, to see if any of them sold that same model of work boot.

Walmart was the only chain that carried it.

By five p.m. all five of the managers had called to report that, during the time specified on that Tuesday, no one had bought a pair of those boots in any size.

After the fifth phone call, Snow snapped his cell phone shut, set it on Alice's desk, and leaned back in his swivel chair.

"Fuck," he said. "We're dead in the water."

"Not yet," Alice said.

"What do you mean 'not yet'?" Snow asked.

"There are fifteen more Walmarts in the Las Vegas area."

"You want to check all of them?" Snow said, staring at her in disbelief.

"Yes," Alice said. "She might have assumed, correctly, that the homicide investigators assigned to the case would only check the stores nearest her residence. That only makes sense. Right?"

"Right," Snow agreed.

"Then we will do what doesn't make sense. We'll check all twenty Walmarts."

Snow stared at her, frowning. "Today?"

"Yes," Alice said. "We have enough time. We'll split up. You take seven. I'll take eight."

"What about dinner?" Snow asked.

"It'll be late," Alice said. "We should be done by ten."

"The buffets will be closed before then," Snow said. "And this sounds like a real long shot. My gut feeling is that this is a waste of time."

Alice sighed. "Alright, Jim. You cover as many as you can, and I'll take the rest. I don't want you to go hungry."

Snow chuckled and shook his head. "Alright. I'll take eight, Alice. You take seven."

"I'll flip you for it," Alice said.

Alice covered the south and east, Snow the west and north.

He was making good time and had organized his procedure by calling ahead to speak with each of the store managers before he got there. This enabled him to meet each manager near the front doors, explain what he needed, and hand the manager the photos of Crystal. And then call the next one.

At eight fifteen, in North Las Vegas, Snow was jogging back to his car when his cell phone chirped. He slowed to a walk, pulled it out, and checked the number.

"Alice," he said. "I'm doing really good. Only two left."

"I'm doing better," Alice said. "We just hit the jackpot!"

"What?" Snow stopped walking. He stopped breathing.

She sounded out of breath. "I just got a call from one of the stores on Eastern Avenue. They identified Crystal Olson purchasing that same pair of boots, size twelve, at four thirty-five p.m. on the fourteenth. They've got clear video of her picking the boots out, and again at the checkout counter. The manager said he'll print out a dozen photos of her. We can pick them up in fifteen minutes at the entrance. I'll meet you there in front of the shopping carts."

CHAPTER 36

Alice James sat erect at her desk, her forearms resting on the arm supports of her swivel chair, her fingers interlaced.

Jim Snow escorted their guests into her office and seated them in the client chairs across from Alice. He then seated himself in his swivel chair at the end of Alice's desk and crossed his arms.

Alice's voice was calm, the words flowing evenly. "Thank you for coming by so late in the evening on such short notice," she said. "We appreciate that. But this is very important. We have something urgent we need to discuss with Crystal."

Crystal Olson sat with her hands in her lap, her shoulders limp. She watched Alice's face with glassy eyes, her eyebrows drawn together and her mouth hanging open. Her mother, Kathy, sat next to her with an identical expression. Neither of them spoke.

"Crystal," Alice said, "you told us that after you got off work on the fourteenth, you went shopping."

"That's right," Crystal said.

"Do you mind telling us where you went shopping?"

She shrugged. "Meadows Mall."

"Did you buy anything there?" Alice said.

Crystal shook her head. "I tried on a few things at Macy's. Decided I didn't like them."

"Did you buy any shoes?" Alice said.

Crystal's eyes widened, along with her mouth. "No. Why?"

Alice opened her bottom desk drawer, lifted the work boots out, and set them on the desk. They landed with a solid thud.

"Did you buy any boots like these, Crystal?" Alice asked.

Crystal and her mother stared at the boots as if they were a basket full of squirming snakes.

"No," she said, her voice a dry rasp.

"How about at Walmart—on Eastern Avenue?"

Crystal said nothing. She continued to stare at the boots, her face losing color.

Alice opened the drawer in front of her. She reached inside for the stack of photos and pulled them out. She set them on the desk. "You might want to look through these," Alice said. "In case you forgot where you went shopping and what you bought."

Alice picked them up and moved them to the far side of the desk in front of Crystal.

Crystal and her mother stared at the top photo. It was a clear printout of Crystal standing in front of the size twelve men's shoe rack, examining a pair of the brown work boots.

Finally Crystal spoke. "Okay. So I bought a pair of men's boots. They were a gift for my fiancé."

"Where are they?" Alice asked. "Can you show them to us?"

"Huh?"

"Where are the boots you bought from this store?"

She stared at Alice as though in shock. She said nothing.

Kathy Olson finally spoke, her words rushed. "Alright. How much do you want for these pictures—this information?" Her eyes shifted from the pictures to Alice, then Jim, and back to Alice.

Alice leaned forward slightly. "This isn't for sale, Kathy."

"The reason we asked Crystal to stop by," Snow piped up, "is to show her what we now know. These pictures were taken at four thirty-five p.m. on the fourteenth of September, not long before Laura Roberts's corpse was discovered burning near Stober Road. The tread on the boots you bought, Crystal, which are identical to these on the desk, match perfectly the tracks in the dirt near the burn site."

"There must be a reasonable price we can pay for this information," Kathy tried again.

"There isn't," Snow said. "We've concluded our investigation, and as a favor to Crystal, we decided to show her what we know before we turn it over to Metro Homicide. Now, we can wait a reasonable amount of time before we do that. This will allow Crystal, if she wishes, to go to the police with an attorney and tell them everything that happened."

Kathy thrust her hand up, covering her mouth as though she were about to vomit. Crystal's gaze wandered back to the boots. Color began to return to her cheeks, her mouth open as though emitting a silent scream. She stared at them as though they were the remains of her dead roommate.

Kathy covered her face completely with both hands, her eyes squeezed shut.

A few moments passed with everyone frozen in place, no one speaking.

Eventually Kathy Olson removed her hands from her face and sat upright in her chair. She folded her hands together in her lap and stared down at them.

Calmly, she said, "I was afraid this would happen. In a way, I'm relieved it has come out, because now the waiting is over." She turned her head to her daughter. "Crystal, I think it's time to tell the truth."

Crystal's eyes welled up with tears. Crossing her arms, she lowered her head and gazed at the floor.

Kathy raised her head and fixed her eyes on Alice. She took a deep breath and let it out. She said, "I killed Laura Roberts."

Alice's eyes popped wide open. Snow's eyebrows shot up.

"How could that be?" Snow protested. "You were in Omaha."

Kathy shook her head. "I wasn't in Omaha. I was here in Las Vegas."

Snow waited, still overwhelmed by her statement, his heart racing.

"I flew down here to visit Crystal on the fourteenth. I was expecting to arrive in the evening, but they put me on an earlier flight. I knew Crystal would still be at work, so I didn't want to bother her there. I decided to surprise her. Instead, I surprised someone else."

She settled back in her chair, swallowed hard, and continued. "I got a taxi from the airport and arrived at her home shortly after two in the afternoon. I have my own key to Crystal's front door for situations like this, where I need to get in when she isn't there.

"So, I let myself in. Quietly, because I knew Laura worked the swing shift and I didn't want to wake her, should she be sleeping.

"I went into the living room and set my bags down. And heard strange noises coming from down the hallway. I had never heard anything like it. It sounded like a woman being tortured.

"I decided to investigate, and so I walked quietly down the hallway to Laura's room, since it was becoming apparent to me the noises were coming from there.

"The door to her bedroom was wide open. And I stood in the doorway staring in horror at the two of them."

"Who?" Snow asked.

Kathy looked at Snow. "Laura Roberts and Andrew Tully, my daughter's fiancé. They were in Laura's bed, completely without clothes, doing things to each other that I have never seen before. I was both horrified and disgusted at the same time. And I screamed at them."

She stopped. Alice and Snow waited.

Kathy lowered her gaze to her hands in her lap. "Well, they stopped what they'd been doing and stared back at me with the same amount of horror I was feeling, I'm sure. They jumped out of bed and began putting on clothes, both of them cursing.

"Andrew didn't even have his shoes on. He went running out of there, barefoot, without even a hello or good-bye. Like I was a ghost or something."

She raised her gaze to Alice. "Once Andrew was out of there, I confronted Laura about the situation in her bedroom. I asked her how she could do such a thing with her best friend's fiancé, of all people.

"We argued. Heatedly. Began yelling at each other. I was so mad I just wanted to grab her by the hair and beat her senseless head against the wall." Kathy clenched her teeth together so tightly her jaw muscles popped out. She stared fire at Alice. "The things that woman said to me, I couldn't believe. The names she called me. Vile, horrible things. And the look on her face as she said them. All I wanted to do at that moment was kill her."

"How did it happen?" Alice said.

Kathy nodded. "Somehow I calmed myself down. At least I thought I had. I walked out of her bedroom and went into the living room. Laura slammed her bedroom door so loud the whole house shook. Then I saw the bat leaning against the corner near the front door. I wasn't even thinking about what I was doing. I just walked over to it and picked it up." She paused, her eyes filling with tears.

"Take your time," Alice said.

Kathy nodded. Her eyes focused on the front of Alice's desk, she continued. "I walked back over to the end of the hallway and stood behind the wall near the corner of it. And I called to her, in a friendly voice, and told her I wanted to talk to her for a moment. She yelled back for me to leave, and I told her I would, but I wanted to apologize before I left."

"Apologize for what?" Alice said.

Kathy shrugged. "For invading her privacy. That's what I told her, and it worked. She came out of her room, down the hallway. And when I saw her head emerge past the corner and into the living room—I swung that bat with every ounce of strength I had in me." She looked at Snow. "I'm sorry, Jim. Could I trouble you for some water?"

Snow jumped up and left the office. He returned a minute later carrying three cups full of water. He handed one to Crystal, another to Kathy, and set the third in front of Alice. The three women thanked him. He pulled his spiral notebook out of his back pocket and sat down. He began to write.

Kathy drank half the water in her cup. She lowered it to her lap and held it there with both hands as she continued. "Well," she said, "after I hit her with the bat, I immediately regretted it, but it was too late for that. She fell over, knocking the lamp off the end table, and took a few strained breaths. And that was it. Suddenly the life was gone from her. I knew immediately she was dead. And I just stood there, with the bat still in my hands, staring down at her. Suddenly I was overcome with an urge to vomit. I was thinking, *I hope I don't throw up on her.* Fortunately I didn't.

"I went and put the bat back from where I had gotten it and sat down on the couch. And I was still sitting there when Crystal walked in."

"What were you thinking while you were sitting there?" Alice said.

"I considered calling 911," Kathy said. "But I knew if I did that, I'd be going to jail, and then prison. And then I realized that my life was over. After that I didn't really think about anything. I was in a daze until Crystal got home. And when she walked in, I think she went into shock too. She didn't say anything to me. Just stood there looking at Laura lying on the floor.

"Finally I came to my senses and told Crystal to leave. I would get rid of the body and straighten up. But Crystal wanted to help me. She's always been a good daughter."

"Whose idea was it to buy the work boots?" Snow asked.

Crystal finally spoke up. "That was my idea. I thought it would throw the police off track if we took the body out into the desert and burned it to get rid of any evidence. And if there were footprints left there by a man, that would lead them away from my mother. The problem, I knew, would be with the ground being so hard. It might not leave any footprints. So we stopped along the way to scrape up some loose dirt with a shovel. I thought if we put some of that down in a few places, there would be some obvious prints for the police to use as evidence."

"Then why did you cover the footprints later?" Snow asked.

"We started to think that maybe it wasn't such a good idea to leave such obvious prints. I was afraid the police might trace the soles of the shoes. And that's what you did."

"Whose car did you use?" Snow said.

"Laura's," Crystal said. "We carried the body out to the garage and put her in the back seat. That was the reason I knew I had to help. My mother couldn't get the body out to the car by herself without dragging it. I was afraid of her leaving evidence behind, and it just seemed too gross to me."

"Who dragged the body out away from the road?" Snow said.

"I did," Kathy said. "I wore the men's boots. I set the body on fire. All Crystal did was help me carry the body to the car."

"And she bought the shoes," Alice said.

"I wanted to be the one to go buy them," Kathy said. "But I don't know my way around Las Vegas very well—"

"I wanted to pick a store on the other side of town," Crystal said, "so it wouldn't be a likely place for the police to check. So I went and got the boots while my mother stayed with the body."

"What did you do after you got back from Stober Road?" Snow asked.

"I took my mother to a motel," Crystal said. "Got her checked in. Then I went home and called the police to report the disturbance in the living room."

Snow continued to scribble in his tiny notebook.

"What about Erin Potter?" Alice asked. "Did she have a role in this?"

Crystal's eyes narrowed. "Erin? She didn't even know about it."

"She tried to get her hairstylist to provide an alibi for her," Alice said. "Why would she do that?"

Crystal shrugged. "I have no idea."

"What about your fiancé?"

"He's no longer my fiancé," Crystal said. "That's definitely over."

"He must have come to some conclusions about what happened in your home after he left," Alice suggested.

"He probably thought I killed Laura," Crystal said.

"You didn't think he might talk to the police?" Snow said.

"Not likely," Crystal said. "He's not the type to want to get involved. And I know he cares about me. I don't think he'd want to see me go to prison."

No one spoke for a moment.

Then Kathy ended the silence. "So what do we do now? We've told you everything. As you can see, this was a horrible thing, but it wasn't planned. There is nothing evil about it. Is there any chance of just keeping this to yourselves? You could report to your client that you weren't able to uncover anything. I could pay you double or even triple what you'll earn from your client. What purpose will it serve for me to go to prison?"

"I'm sorry," Snow said. "But we don't work that way. We need to stay within the law. We can't cover up evidence."

"If you don't say anything," Kathy insisted, "that's not covering anything up."

"It is," Snow said. "But I'm not going to argue that issue. Here's what we'll do. Tomorrow afternoon at two p.m. we'll call the lead homicide investigator to check on his progress in the case. If he tells us that you turned yourself in, we'll congratulate him on resolving the case, and we'll issue a report to our client based on what he tells us. Nothing more. That will be the end of it. This should give you enough time to contact an attorney and tell him that you've decided to do the right thing."

"What will happen to Crystal?" Kathy asked.

"I can't say," Snow replied. "But my guess is that the DA won't bother with charges against her. And your charges will be greatly reduced once your lawyer has a chance to negotiate the sentence."

"I don't have a lawyer," Kathy said.

"I can give you a short list," Snow said. "Alright? How does that sound to you?"

The women nodded solemnly. Tears ran down Crystal's cheeks.

"Okay," Snow said. "Good luck to you."

They got up slowly. Alice and Snow escorted them to the front door. They watched the women climb into Crystal's car. She backed it out of the parking space and slowly drove away.

Standing in the open doorway, Alice said, "What are you thinking, Jim?"

Snow sighed. "You're always asking me that. I think this profession reminds me a lot of playing poker for a living."

"In what way?"

"We make our money," Snow said, "at the expense of other people."

"Not always," Alice said. "But I was thinking how easy it would be to ruin your entire life with one moment of bad judgment."

"You still want to smack me on the head?" Snow asked.

"Yes," Alice said. "I do."

She turned toward him and kissed him on the jaw.

"That wasn't so bad," Snow said.

CHAPTER 37

"What are you going to have?" Alice said.

"What do I always have?" Snow said.

"Ham, eggs, white toast, and waffles," Alice said.

"Well," Snow said, "this time I'm having something different. I've been giving it some thought, ever since our encounter with that psychologist."

Alice took a sip of coffee. "Really. That's encouraging. What sort of changes did you have in mind?"

Snow set his menu down on the table in front of him and leaned back in his chair. "First of all, I'm going to try very hard to get us some new business."

"And what will that entail?"

"I don't know," Snow said. "You've already sent out marketing letters to every lawyer in Clark County. Maybe I'll get some T-shirts and caps printed up."

Alice chuckled. "What else?"

"Furthermore," Snow said, "I plan to dress better from now on. You may have noticed today my shirt is tucked in."

"I did notice," Alice said. "That's commendable. I'm impressed. So what are you having to eat?"

"Steak, eggs, wheat toast, and waffles."

"This is exciting," Alice said. "I'll have to make an entry in my diary."

Out of the corner of his eye, Snow noticed the owner of the restaurant approaching their table. He was a gangly Norwegian in his mid-forties with a full head of thick brown hair. He wore gray slacks, a white shirt with the sleeves rolled up, and a burgundy tie.

"Eddie," Snow said. "How's business?"

Eddie stopped in front of their window booth. He grinned. "Good," he said. "I haven't seen you two in here for a while. I was afraid something happened to you."

"Something happened to us all right," Snow said. "I don't know if it's the recession or my lack of business sense. It's been slow for us. We've had to cut back on our expenses."

"Well, this one is on the house," Eddie said. "Your money's no good here."

"That's nice of you, Eddie," Snow said. "But we insist on paying our way."

"You can pay if you want," Eddie said. "I'll just tear up the receipt. No sense arguing about it."

"Alright," Snow said. "You win this one, but you'll have to agree to bring Georgine over to dinner one night. Alice is planning to make some lutefisk."

Eddie scowled. "Aghh, I hate that stuff."

Snow chuckled and slapped the table. "You're from Bismarck and you don't like lutefisk?"

"You're from Minnesota," Eddie said. "You like it?"

Snow screwed up his face and shook his head.

"Alright, alright," Alice said. "We'll grill some chicken instead."

"Oh, hey," Eddie said. "I finally did it. I finally hired some-body named Wanda. She's a new cook, just started Monday."

"So Wanda's Waffle House is legitimate," Snow said.

Eddie laughed.

Snow's cell phone chirped.

Eddie raised his hand. "I gotta get back to work," he said, and then he wandered off.

Snow pulled his phone out and put it to his ear. "Yeah, Mel. What's up?"

"Magnum P.I.—how's the gumshoe business?"

"Terrible," Snow said.

"Well," Harris said, "I've got some good news and some bad."

"You got some strange woman pregnant," Snow guessed.

Harris laughed. "First I'd have to get one…oh, wait…let me write that down. That's a keeper."

"So what happened?" Snow asked.

"That case you've been investigating has come to a close."

"You're kidding. You solved it?"

"No," Harris said. "The perp came in and confessed."

"Really. Who is he?"

"It's not a *he*. It's a *she*," Harris said. "Kathren Olson, the mother of the victim's roommate. She says they had an argu-ment, and she ended it by knocking her head out of the park."

"I didn't know she was even in town," Snow said.

"Yeah," Harris said. "I don't why she confessed. We would have never tied her to the crime."

"I know what you mean," Snow said.

"Well, anyway. The chief's planning to issue a press release after lunch. So you can probably bill a few more hours until then."

"Thanks, Mel," Snow said. "That's good to know."

"Say hello to your partner for me," Harris said. "Tell her I think she ought to make you an honest man."

"Now you're scaring me," Snow said.

"Tell me about it," Harris said. "Take care."

Snow flipped his phone shut and shoved it in his pocket.

"So that's done," Alice said.

"Yep," Snow said. "I figured they'd do the right thing."

"I still wonder about Erin Potter," Alice said. "Why would she go to the trouble of trying to create an alibi when she had nothing to do with the murder?"

Snow took a swallow of coffee and set the cup down. "She was probably afraid of getting sucked into the mess by association. Innocent people go to jail all the time."

"You know what else I was wondering about?" Alice said.

"What's that?"

"Kathy Olson's murdered husband. I wonder if she had anything to do with it."

Snow nodded. "I've been thinking about that myself. We'll never get the answer to that question."

"Oh!" Alice said. "I forgot to tell you. My sister Corina called me again last night. She's definitely coming to meet me this weekend." Her face spread into a grin. "She'll be driving down here from San Jose on Friday. She said she'll be leaving work at noon."

"She doesn't want to fly? That must be five hundred miles."

"She said she hates airports," Alice said. "She loves to drive, and she just got a new car. I'm so excited. I can't believe I'm finally going to meet her."

Snow smiled and nodded.

"And I want you to meet her too," Alice said. "Maybe the three of us can have dinner together somewhere Saturday night. Someplace nice."

"I'll have to wear something snazzy," Snow said. "I think I have an expensive dress shirt somewhere in my closet. Hopefully I can remember how to work the iron."

END

About the Author

Photograph by Geraldine Cowden, 2010

Rex Kusler was born in Missouri and raised in a small town in Iowa. Thanks to a lifelong fascination with mathematical probability and gambling, he enjoys spending his free time in Las Vegas and looks forward to retiring there. For now, he lives and works in the Bay Area of northern California, seeking humor and fun in whatever he does.